THE LIFE COACH

A Lesbian Romance

Sienna Waters

Find out more at:

www.siennawaters.com

To N.–

My one and only
xxx

CHAPTER ONE

Alice winced as the brush caught in her hair. "Ninety seven," she said. "Ninety eight," as the brush traveled down again.

"Knock knock." Harrison stood in the doorway, a steaming mug in either hand.

Two more half-hearted strokes and Alice put the hairbrush neatly in its place on the dressing table and then grinned. "Cocoa? For real?"

Harrison rolled her eyes. "You know I actually think 'for real' every damn time I see you," she said, taking a couple of steps to hand Alice a mug before perching on the end of the bed.

"And why's that?"

"Um... You actually have an outfit ready and hanging on the back of your chair for tomorrow morning," Harrison said. "Your dressing table looks like you tidied it with a ruler and set-square in your hand. You literally just gave your hair a hundred strokes with a hairbrush, and don't deny it, I heard you counting."

"What's wrong with that?" Alice asked, tucking her now very shiny blonde hair behind her ears.

Harrison sighed. "You're... I don't know, you're like one of those dolls, the big ones, what are they called? American Girl dolls, you know the ones I mean?"

Alice had a brief memory of the four American Girl dolls that were currently in storage at her parents' place and blushed.

"Mm-hmm," she said.

"And you have... what is that exactly?" Harrison asked, pointing to what was hung on the wall next to the dressing table.

"A mood board."

"For what?"

Alice felt the blush creeping further up her face. "Um, for stuff."

Harrison leaned in to take a closer look. "Is that a wedding dress?"

"Uh..."

"Kind of my point, Al. You're special. Not like anyone else I know. Not that that's a bad thing," Harrison added quickly. "You're lovely and wonderful and amazing. I just don't think I've met anyone else whose goal in life is to become a wife."

"That's not my goal in life," Alice protested even though secretly she kind of thought it might be. At least a little.

"You want the fairy tale," Harrison said, crossing her legs. "I get it. It's just that most women I know don't believe in fairy tales anymore."

"Well that's on them," said Alice. "And you're the one bringing hot cocoa to my room."

"Yeah, I thought you'd appreciate the touch," Harrison grinned. She lifted her mug, baring a wrist and the swirling colors of her tattoos. "Especially on the night before your big day and all."

"It's not that important," Alice said, though her stomach clenched a little.

"Your first day on the job, that's pretty important, roomie. And didn't you say the guy's famous?"

Alice bit her lip and nodded. "He's a big deal," she admitted.

"A big deal in the world of... life coaching?"

She double checked Harrison's face, but she didn't seem to be teasing. They'd been roommates for six months now and Alice adored Harrison. Technically, she'd nursed a crush on the older woman right up until Harrison had quashed it by being straight, but once dreams of a white wedding were out of the picture,

Alice had come to love her in other ways.

She wasn't always sure when Harrison was teasing though. Not that the fiercely protective red-head was mean, just sometimes she let her wicked sense of humor and her sharp tongue get away from her.

"Life coaching," Alice agreed.

"Which is... what exactly?" Harrison sipped from the mug then pulled a face. "Jesus, this is disgusting."

"What were you expecting?" Alice frowned. "You're the one who made it."

"I don't know. I thought it'd be like hot chocolate or something," Harrison grimaced.

Alice took a drink then nearly spat it out. "You forgot the sugar," she said. "Have you never had cocoa before?"

Harrison shook her head. "I thought it sounded appropriately sweet and innocent and like something you'd like," she said. "So I grabbed some from the store. Guess I probably should have read the instructions."

"Probably," Alice said, glad for the distraction. Not that she didn't want to answer Harrison's question. It was more that she couldn't. She actually had no idea what Foster Davison, her new boss, did. Other than make YouTube videos and visit clients.

Not that she hadn't tried. But his website was big on motivational mottoes and slim on details. Still though, she was only supposed to be his assistant. She'd figure things out.

"Okay, I'm getting rid of this swill," Harrison said. "Hand that cup over."

Alice did as she was told.

"Oh." Harrison turned as she got to the door. "And you'd better figure out what the hell life coaching is," she added. "We've got rent to pay, and we need your fancy new job to pay it."

Alice smiled with more confidence than she really felt. "It's all gonna be fine."

She really hoped that it would be.

She heard Harrison clomping down the hallway to the kitchen and her eyes caught on the mood board.

Ms. Right was a long time coming, if she was even out there. Not that Alice didn't want to achieve other things in life. Of course she did. But her dreams, even as a kid, had been about having a house, a partner, raising children. It was what she wanted, old-fashioned or not.

Sometimes she worried that she'd been born a half-century too late.

In the kitchen the microwave beeped and then Harrison swore long and loud. Alice shook her head and went to make sure that her roommate hadn't burned herself too badly.

THE OFFICES WERE all glass and white walls and Alice felt herself calming a little as she sat primly in the waiting room. Neat and tidy, perfectly ordered, this was her kind of place.

Her shoes were shined, her bag was on her lap, she had every reason to be confident.

Except she could see a woman talking to the receptionist and both were looking in her direction. Her heart sank just a little.

"I'm Alice Knowles," she'd introduced herself to the receptionist. "I'm Foster Davison's new assistant."

And the look on the woman's face had told her all she needed to know. A mixture of fear and pity. Alice's mouth went dry at the memory of it.

All of this was a mistake, she could see that now.

Okay, she needed a job. And this had seemed kind of perfect. 'Well-organized, efficient and charming assistant required.' The sentence could have been written about her.

But the first red flag should have been the fact that she'd been interviewed by a woman. A woman with dark hair who'd asked all the questions and given her a frosty smile. Not Foster himself. In fact, she hadn't even heard his name until the interview was over.

She definitely hadn't actually met him.

She uncrossed her legs then re-crossed them in the other direction. If he was that bad, then she'd quit, she told herself. Life was too short for a job she was going to hate.

She checked the clock behind the vast reception desk. The guy obviously needed an assistant. He was already fifteen minutes late. She sighed and tried to relax her face so that she didn't look irritated.

"Mr. Davison will be with you shortly," the receptionist called over.

Alice smiled politely.

He'd better.

Or...

Or she'd walk, she told herself, knowing that she'd never find the courage to do so.

But she could dream. She half-closed her eyes, imagining the satisfaction of getting up, smoothing down her skirt, striding out of the offices, the receptionist calling after her.

"Knowles!"

The word was barked across the waiting room. She opened her eyes. A short man with sallow skin and an expensive suit was standing impatiently by a glass door.

"Get a move on then," he said, glancing her over from top to toe in one look.

"Mr. Davison," she began.

"I don't have time for pleasantries, get a move on, time is money here and I'm a very busy man."

He turned and strode down the corridor and Alice had to run to catch the glass door before it closed and locked her back out in the waiting room. She hurried after him.

"Coffee on my desk at nine sharp when I'm in the office," he said. "All calls are screened, no matter who they're from. I'm out of the office or unavailable to everyone. If it's important I'll call them back. Keep things neat and tidy, ensure my calendar is up to date and don't even think about using those horrific little sticky post-it bookmarks that look like arrows. I can't stand the fuckers."

Alice was practically running to keep up with him, fervently wishing that she could take notes.

"You'll be in here," he said, pushing open a door. "My office is the door behind you, I expect you in by eight thirty and at your desk until at least five, though some days you'll stay longer, don't talk back, don't contradict me, address me as 'sir.' Any questions?"

Alice gulped. "Uh, how do you take your coffee?" She saw his eyebrow raise and hastily added a 'sir' to the end of her question.

"Black," he said, and let go of the door he was holding so that it slammed in her face so close that she felt it brush past her nose.

He disappeared into his own office, slamming the door, and leaving Alice feeling an awful lot like she'd been picked up by a tornado and deposited somewhere that very definitely wasn't Kansas anymore.

CHAPTER TWO

Viv yanked at Max's leash, pulling him back from the grass at the edge of the park.

"I swear to all the gods, Max, you roll in poop again and you're cleaning your own damn self up."

Max wagged his tail enthusiastically and Viv sighed, pulling the dog along in her wake.

"Time we got you home. Come on then, let's get going."

Max trotted obediently alongside her, ignoring the temptations of the children's park, the soccer field, and even the odd piece of interesting trash along the route. In general, he was a good-natured animal if not always the most well-behaved.

"You know, you're the most sensible conversation I get all day," Viv said as they walked back out onto the street. Which was mostly true, if only because Max was often the only one she talked to all day.

Max whined, sensing an opportunity.

"Yeah, yeah, yeah, you'll get your treats when we get home. As long as you behave until then."

She marched with the dog up the street and couldn't help but pat his shaggy head as he stuck to her side.

He wasn't her dog.

Not that she didn't look after him, feed him, walk him, groom him, and all the rest. But technically he wasn't her dog. It had been Bill who'd insisted that a life in the suburbs wasn't complete without a dog.

She'd put her foot down, thinking about the extra work of cleaning dog hair off everything three times a day, and then one evening Bill had appeared with Max in his arms and the deal was done.

Bill being Bill of course, the thrill of having a dog had worn off after a couple of weeks, and Viv had found herself Max's main caretaker. Something she begrudged Bill for, but not enough that she was willing to do anything about it.

After all, Max *was* the most sensible conversation partner she had most of the time. And he didn't mind watching infinite true crime shows on Discovery. Nor did he object to eating cereal for dinner when she'd forgotten the grocery order again.

There were certainly worse roommates in the world.

The house was in the middle of the block, a pale yellow, one-floor ranch with shutters for the windows and a tree in the backyard big enough for a rope swing. The tree had sealed the sale for Bill, obviously. Viv just raked up the leaves every fall and swore.

On either side were houses that looked pretty much the same in different colors and Viv thought that if she ever went color-blind she'd be a bit fucked when it came to finding her way home again. Fucked because that's the kind of woman she was. One that used the F word liberally and refused to be ashamed of it.

There was enough else in her life to worry about that an extra 'fuck' or three a day wasn't going to bother her.

She was walking up the driveway when Max pulled away from her to investigate something in the grass.

"What's that?"

Max looked up at her with a guilty grin on his face, tongue lolling out. Viv grunted, got down on her knees and pulled a small child's shovel out of the long grass. She swore and tossed it as far as she could over into next door's yard.

Mr. Webber from next door spoiled his grandchildren and let them run riot. She'd complained multiple times but the man just laughed and told her to lighten up. Which made her want to light him up.

Unfortunately, Mr. Webber was currently weeding a front flowerbed, hidden by a bush, and the shovel flew into his yard and clunked against something.

"What the—"

A bald head emerged from behind the bush. Mr. Webber rubbed at said bald head and glanced down at the bright red shovel lying on the lawn then back up at Viv.

"Did you just throw a spade at me?"

Viv grunted and pulled at Max's leash. Max sat down, refusing to move, tongue out and panting. He quite liked Mr. Webber, who occasionally fed him pieces of meat from his backyard grill when Viv wasn't looking.

"Damn right I did," Viv said, putting her hands on her hips. If she was going to have this conversation then she might as well take the offensive. "And you'd better keep those kids out of my yard."

Mr. Webber snorted. "Seriously? They're four and six. You don't even have a fence up. What's it to you if they stray over the property line every now and again? It's not like they're peeking in your windows or anything."

"It's private property," Viv said. "Keep them off my lawn."

"You need to lighten up, lady," said Mr. Webber.

Viv had a momentary image of setting a match to Mr. Webber and seeing his face flickering behind flames as he mouthed the words 'lighten up.' "You need to respect private property," she said. "If I see them on my lawn again, I'll call the police."

Mr. Webber muttered something under his breath.

"What was that?" Viv said, hands still on hips.

"Nothing."

"I thought not." She pulled at Max's lead one more time and this time the dog finally gave in to the lure of treats inside the house.

She carefully unlocked the door, unclasped Max's lead to let him run free, then stepped inside and locked the door behind her with a sigh of relief.

That was her done for the day.

Okay, it was only half past ten, but she'd taken care of her responsibilities. Max was walked. She'd let him out into the back yard later for a run around and a pee before bed, but other than that, she was free and clear.

The living room opened up off the hallway. She dropped her keys in a bowl on a side table and looked longingly at the nest of blankets on the couch. Blankets, couch, TV. The call of the afternoon half-coma was strong.

She was about to get herself settled when she caught a whiff of stale body odor. Eugh. Okay, a shower first. One more responsibility.

Then it was time to do nothing.

Her favorite thing to do.

She had no idea how other people managed hobbies. She barely had time for walking Max, complaining at the kids on the lawn, and watching her shows. And she didn't even work. How the hell other people went mountain climbing or did crochet or whatever else was beyond her.

She peeled her t-shirt and jeans off in the hall, leaving them where they lay, before heading into the bedroom and the connected bathroom.

The shower took forever to run hot and with Max snuffling around in his food bowl, there was no one to distract her from herself.

So Viv took a long, hard look in the mirror.

Short, dark, messy hair, blue eyes dark as denim. Her arms were a tad too chubby, but her waist was slim, and her boobs still perky. Not bad for an old woman, she thought to herself as steam began to crawl from the shower.

Old.

Thirty five wasn't old.

It just felt that way.

It felt that way when she looked around her and realized that...

She sighed, gritting her teeth and climbing into the shower.

Nobody lived the perfect life, she reminded herself as she soaped up. Nobody had the life they'd dreamed of. She certainly wasn't alone in this.

The sound of the phone ringing startled her so much that she got shampoo in her eye and swore yet again as she grabbed a towel and plunged out of the shower. Frantically rubbing at her eye she bumped into the doorframe and registered her seventh 'fuck' of the day before finally getting the phone next to the bed.

"What?"

"Jeez, aren't we all sunshine and light this morning?"

"Jesus, Evie, I thought you were the plumber calling me back. What do you want?"

"Has anyone ever told you that your phone manner could use a little work?" Evie said.

Viv sniffed. Manners were for suckers. She'd learned that one the hard way. "What do you want?"

"I'm coming over."

"There's no one home."

"Ha ha, very funny. You told me I should call before I visit, so I'm abiding by your wishes. I'm coming over."

Viv saw her afternoon plans spiraling away down the drain. Blankets. Couch. TV. Then she sighed. "When?"

There was a pause. Then the doorbell sounded. "Surprise," said Evie-on-the-phone, but Viv could see the shadow of Evie-at-the-front-door waving madly through the glass.

She groaned, hung up, and rooted around for some sweats to put on.

CHAPTER THREE

Alice was re-ordering the files on the top of a filing cabinet when the door behind her swung open.

"Good. A tidy environment leads to a tidy mind," Foster said approvingly. He was carrying a buff-colored folder. He walked past her desk and around to the door into the corridor. "Walk with me," he said as he went out.

Alice gulped, grabbed a pen and notepad from her desk and rushed after him.

"The number one most important thing that you have to remember," Foster was saying as she caught up with him. "Is that the clients are the priority here. Win a client over and that client will tell three people on average how impressed he is with my services. Lose a client and that client will go on to tell tens, possibly hundreds of people how bad I am at what I do."

Which meant that the priority here wasn't exactly the clients. It was making Foster Davison look good. Alice didn't write this down. She made a humming noise that she hoped Foster would see as agreement. They stopped in front of an elevator.

"Many of my clients are repeaters," he said, as the door slid open and he got in.

Alice hesitated for only a second before getting in with him.

"Which means we need to continually keep them satisfied."

There was a brief pause and Alice looked up. Foster still looked sallow, not at all like he did in his videos. But then, she guessed, that was the power of make-up.

"Believe it or not, keeping a client satisfied does not mean giving them an immediate appointment," Foster said now.

Alice wrote it down. No immediate appointments.

"Many of the people that I see are one percenters. They're not used to waiting, and part of what I teach them involves waiting," Foster said. "Which means giving them immediate appointments is counter-productive."

Alice wrote 'counter-productive' and underlined it twice.

"What if it's an emergency?" she asked, unsure if life coaches had emergencies.

Foster stared at her, his eyes narrowing. His hair was gelled back to show a distinct widow's peak. "Excellent question," he said after a heart-stalling moment. The elevator stopped, he got out, Alice followed.

They were marching toward the exit. It might have been an excellent question, but apparently Foster wasn't intending to answer it. He opened the outside door, striding through it and leaving Alice to follow in his wake.

It was only when they were outside on the street, the breeze cutting through her thin blouse, that Alice cleared her throat. "Um, where are we going?"

Foster glared at her. "To lunch," he said. "Keep up."

Alice cast a look back at the office where she'd left her jacket, then sighed and jogged for a couple of steps to catch up with her boss.

THE RESTAURANT WAS all tiny plates and people who'd rather be seen than actually eat anything and Alice's stomach rumbled as the waiter poured mineral water for them both.

"I expect you to keep a close eye on my diary, and to be able to give me a briefing on new clients before I meet them," Foster was saying, ignoring the waiter completely. "On that note, this is our next client." He slid the buff-colored folder over to her. "I'm meeting her directly after lunch."

Alice opened the folder and found a single piece of paper with a name typed at the top and an address under it. She looked back at Foster with a frown.

"That's what happens when someone doesn't do their job properly, and that's why you've now got that job," Foster said, a look of satisfaction on his face. A look that momentarily slipped as he paled slightly.

"Are you okay?" Alice asked.

"Fine," snapped Foster. "In the future, I expect a full dossier on any potential client. That will be your job."

Alice nodded. She bit back any reply she might have been going to make. Her morning hadn't been wasted. She'd spent the time re-ordering files, snooping through the computer on her desk, and generally getting the lay of the land.

And she'd come to one, very solid conclusion. Foster Davison wasn't as successful as he wanted people to believe. He might have been in the past, she'd found tons of old client files, but there'd been next to nothing over the last three months.

She was beginning to understand why Foster was quite so irritable.

"What can I get for you?" the waiter asked, sidling up to the table.

"We'll both take the house salad," Foster said, picking up both menus and handing them back. "Make it fast."

The waiter disappeared off and Alice was coming to another very solid conclusion. This job was not for her. Foster Davison was a rude, arrogant, little man who was going to be a pill to be around. Not the kind of atmosphere that Alice was looking for at all.

There was still one little thing that was bugging her though.

"What exactly does a life coach do?" she asked, leaning forward.

Foster laughed, then grimaced and paled again for a moment.

"I teach people how to live," he said. "I take those who are lost, lonely, broken, or just plain bored and teach them how to live again."

Which didn't sound all that bad put that way, Alice thought. Maybe she was being too quick to judge her boss.

"I make them face their fears, I make them relive their tragedies, I make them whole and happy again."

She was smiling now. This was something she could get behind. And Foster was grinning right back at her, leaning forward now, almost confidentially.

"And most importantly," he said. "I take their money."

Alice felt her smile sliding away. But before she could say anything, Foster grimaced again.

"Are you sure you're alright?" she asked, pushing his glass of water closer to him.

He nodded, but she could see sweat beading on his forehead.

"Because you really, really don't look alright," she added. Please let him be alright. The last thing she needed was a dead boss on her very first day. Not exactly something that looked great on a CV.

"Fine, I'm fine," he said, but his voice was tight and he was starting to hunch over.

"I really don't think that you are," she said, spotting Foster's cell phone on the table beside his plate.

She reached for it and he put out a hand to stop her but she took no notice, sliding her hand and the phone out from under his sweaty, clammy hand.

"I'm fine," he croaked again.

Then he gave a sound somewhere between a squawk and a cough and slid sideways onto the floor. The restaurant erupted into chatter, but Alice was already calling the emergency services.

"IS HE GOING to be okay?" she asked the tall paramedic.

The woman smiled at her. "I'm sure he's going to be fine. There's no sign it's cardiac, nor anything brain related. He's got stomach pain, but there's not much we can tell from that. We'll take good care of him, don't you worry."

Alice looked doubtfully over to where Foster was being strapped onto a stretcher. "He just sort of... collapsed," she said. Then she looked up at the paramedic who had quite enchanting green eyes. "It's my first day," she said.

The paramedic patted her arm and Alice wondered what it would be like to be married to someone who saved lives every day. "We're taking him to the local hospital, he's going to need some tests. But don't worry too much."

Alice glanced over at Foster again. He was struggling to sit up, to take an oxygen mask off his face. She sighed. "Can I talk to him?" He was beckoning at her, trying to get her attention.

"Sure," the paramedic said. "Just for a second though we need to get moving here."

Alice hurried over and Foster picked off his mask as she arrived. "Client," he croaked.

She looked back through the window of the restaurant. She could see the buff folder still on their table. "Don't worry about it," she said. "I'll call and cancel. You just concentrate on getting better."

He clutched at her arm. "No," he hissed. "Client. Important. Go. You go."

She frowned at him. "You want me to go? But I don't..."

He took a deep breath, steeled himself, then said: "Initial questionnaire. In new client folder on computer. Go. Do it."

She shook her head. "Sir, I really don't think..." But he was clutching at her arm so hard she could feel the bones of his fingers and his face was turning a strange buttery-yellow color. "Fine," she said. "Fine, I'll do it."

The stretcher bounced as one of the paramedics pushed it onto the ambulance-lift, and Foster let his mask go, letting it cover his face again, closing his eyes as if in relief.

Alice watched the ambulance doors close, watched the vehicle pull away before turning back to the restaurant. The folder was still on the table. She sighed. What had she just agreed to do?

CHAPTER FOUR

"You can't just show up at someone's front door," Viv said, standing back so that Evie could slide into the hallway.

"I didn't. I called first," Evie said, pausing to drop a kiss on Viv's cheek. "Interesting place to keep dirty clothes. Heard of a thing called a hamper?"

Viv looked down at her jeans and t-shirt in a pile on the floor, rolled her eyes, and kicked them both under the hallway table. "Happy?"

"Always," Evie said. "Let's head in the direction of caffeine."

And she was off to the kitchen, Viv trailing her as though this wasn't her house at all.

Evie had been in Viv's life for about as long as she could remember. She'd been the weird kid with braces next door that Viv's mom had forced her to play with. But over time, a deep and occasionally fierce relationship had sprung up.

They'd got married a week apart, Evie putting off her honeymoon so that she could be Viv's maid of honor. Viv remembered how Evie had grinned at her at the altar, settling her butterflies.

"So, why isn't the coffee machine on?" Evie said.

"Because I didn't know you were coming." Viv flicked the switch and opened up the cupboard to search for filters and coffee.

Evie hadn't stayed weird-looking. She'd bloomed into a tall, dark-haired woman that men honked at in gas stations. And somewhere along the way she'd gotten smart and rich with it until some days, bad days, Viv felt like she might just be living in the cool of Evie's shadow.

Not that Evie would let her get away with thinking that.

Evie was the sister she'd never had. Also never wanted, but that was by the by. They were inextricably connected.

"Tell me everything then," Evie said, once the coffee pot was bubbling and spitting.

"About what?"

"Life," shrugged Evie. "What have you been up to?"

Viv blew out a breath. "I walked Max," she offered, looking over to where the dog snoozed in his basket. Evie was familiar enough that she didn't warrant a full-out barking attack. Max had opened one eye, seen who it was, and fallen back to sleep.

Evie picked up the free newspaper on the counter, collected another and began to make a pile, squaring it off with a satisfying thonk. "Mm-hmm," was all she said.

"I left the house," Viv said defensively. "That was the deal. I left the house this morning. And I've left the house once a day for the last two weeks, no skipping."

"I'm not sure that was really the deal," Evie said. She opened up the mug cabinet, found it empty, and then started to run warm water in the sink to tackle the pile of washing up on the draining board.

"Eve, come on."

Evie switched the water off. "Viv, you come on."

"I—" But there was nothing to say. Viv looked around the kitchen, seeing it with Evie's eyes. Seeing the towering pile of trash on top of the trash can, the washing up not even loaded into the dishwasher, the brochures and junk mail and free papers littered over the surfaces.

Evie turned the water back on, washed out two mugs, poured coffee into both of them, picked them up and walked away. Viv followed her, heart thumping in her chest, knowing that she'd let Evie down.

"Evie, I'm sorry."

Evie pushed plates out of the way and put both coffees down on the living room table. "I've got a surprise."

Anything to change the subject away from just how crap Viv was being at life right now. She managed a grin. "You do? Spill it."

Evie sat on the couch, not bothering to move the blankets away. "A life coach is coming."

And Viv half-fell into the armchair beside the couch. "What?"

"A. Life. Coach. Is. Coming," Evie repeated.

"Hells no," Viv said immediately. "Some woo-woo with crystals and incense and spirits and crap."

Evie frowned. "Yeah, that's not what a life coach is. I think you're thinking of... I don't know. A psychic?"

"Oh."

"A life coach is someone that helps you out of a rut. Someone that gets you back on track, that helps you get your life together, decide what you want."

"I'm not in a rut," Viv said, turning over the idea of a life coach in her head. Okay, essentially it didn't sound that bad. But there were two distinct problems here. "I don't like people telling me what to do."

"Yeah, tell me about it," said Evie, picking up her coffee.

"And I don't want someone just coming into my house and messing with things," she finished. "Private spaces."

"It's a gift," Evie said. "From me. You want to be the kind of person that turns down a gift from your best-est friend in the world?"

"Yeah, that title might be up for grabs pretty soon," Viv grumbled. "I don't need a life coach, Eve."

Evie said nothing, just looked around the living room and Viv groaned. She wasn't stupid. She could see the place from Evie's point of view, and it wasn't good.

"We've been through this, Evie. I'm just... I'm not in a great place."

Evie sighed. "The divorce was final almost a year ago, Viv. At some point, we have to start taking responsibility for this. I'm not asking you to start dating again or anything."

"Good, because that's never going to happen. I mean never. Like, not at all."

"I'm just saying that maybe it's time we asked for a little help."

"I don't want help."

In general, Evie was the happy one, the chirpy one, the one with a smile. But now she rubbed a hand over her face and looked older and tireder than Viv could ever remember seeing her. "I want the old Viv back."

'Too bad,' Viv felt like saying. 'Too bad, she's gone and she can't come back. Not ever.' But she said nothing.

"This can't go on, Viv," Evie said. "You used to be bright and vivacious, the life of the party. You used to have friends."

"I have you."

"You'll always have me," said Evie.

"More's the pity," snorted Viv in a vain attempt to lighten the atmosphere.

"You can't let some asshole take away your life like this, Viv. You can't let Bill change who you are, what you are. That's letting him win."

Okay, that struck a chord. As far as Viv was concerned, she didn't want Bill to win so much as a nickel. But given that he was safe with his new wife on a ranch in California, he was unlikely to care what she wanted.

"Okay, okay, I get that there's a problem here. I get that I need to try harder."

"It's more than trying harder, Viv. You need some help. That's all I'm offering."

"But come on, Eve. A life coach? Really?"

"Why don't you reserve judgment? Start the process and see how you feel? Do the initial interview and then we'll talk about it again?"

Viv bit her lip and Max wandered in from the kitchen, rubbing his head against Viv's hand and then settling down on the rug.

"It's a stupid idea," Viv said.

"Fine, it's a stupid idea. Just try it. For me."

Viv really, really didn't want to do this. Letting a stranger into her life? No way. The problem was, she owed Evie way too much to turn her down. Evie, who had once peeled her off a bathroom floor in a bar in Arizona after an ill-advised experiment with a tequila-jagermeister mix. Evie, who had stood by her side as she got married. Evie, who had grabbed a baseball bat and knocked out all the windows in Bill's car when they found out he was cheating.

Evie had been there for too much, seen too much, for Viv not to do this for her.

For fuck's sake.

"Fine," Viv said.

"Oh, thank God," said Evie.

Viv scowled at her. "That sounded just a little too thankful."

Evie shuffled a little in her seat and Viv's scowl deepened.

"Evie!"

"Okay, okay, I was sure that you were going to say no, so I sort of... took care of things."

Which was why Evie was like a sister to her. Viv couldn't decide if she was touched that Evie cared enough to do this, or if she really wanted to slap her. Probably a combination of both. The door bell rang. Definitely a combination of both, but veering more and more toward the slapping side.

"I'll be off then," Evie said, standing up quickly. "Don't you worry about that, I'll get the door on my way out."

And she was disappearing out into the hall before Viv could say a word.

CHAPTER FIVE

T he house looked nice enough. Actually, the house looked perfectly normal. Not at all what Alice expected based on Foster's website and social media. A little suburban ranch house. Which was just as well, because if it had been a mansion with a curving driveway she might just have backed out completely.

It didn't feel right doing this.

On the other hand, Foster was patently very ill. And she had told him she'd do it.

So she'd do it, she decided, finger pressing the door bell. She'd do it then get the hell out of here and find a whole different kind of job.

Disney, she thought. That should suit her just fine. Smiling and being happy and being surrounded by other smiling, happy people.

She was just wondering whether twenty five was too old to be a Disney princess when the door opened.

"Hi," she said, beaming a big bright smile. "I'm—"

"You're going to be lucky to escape this alive," said the tall woman who opened the door with a grin. "She's in the living room. She's mad. Don't say you haven't been warned. And I'm getting out of here before she realizes I'm completely to blame."

Alice stood aside as the woman pushed past her and watched, confused, as she got into a car. Okay. Obviously not the client then.

Taking a deep breath, she walked into the house itself. Then she wished she'd skipped the deep breath part. The place smelled of old cooking and food, trash and sweat. Not pleasant at all.

"Hello?"

"In here," said a voice.

She followed it into a living room that looked as though someone slept in it. Probably the woman in the armchair, she guessed.

"Uh, you're Vivien Curtis?"

The woman grunted. She was attractive enough, Alice thought. High cheekbones, short hair still wet from a shower and slicked back. She wore sweats, but looked fit under them. Perhaps not a total lost cause then.

Except she didn't exactly know what she was supposed to be looking for.

"Um, I'm Alice Knowles?" She smiled helpfully.

"Yeah, life coach, so I've heard." Vivien sat up a little. "Sit down. Let's get this over with."

A sentiment Alice could get behind. She cleared a little space on the couch and sat down, pulling out Vivien's file and the questionnaire that she'd grabbed from the office.

"Just so you know," Vivien said. "This wasn't my idea."

"Oh." Alice looked down at the form. "Well, this says that it can be filled in by a friend or relative if you prefer?"

The woman scowled and Alice noticed that her eyes were a deep, deep blue. Almost purple. "Hell no, get on with it."

"Fine," said Alice, rather wishing she'd been offered at least a glass of water. Though looking at the state of the house maybe it was better that she hadn't. She looked down at the questionnaire. "Okay, so, what would you say are your main stressors?"

Vivien rolled her eyes and a dog that Alice hadn't noticed growled a little in his sleep. "Getting up in the morning."

"What, sorry?"

"Nothing." The woman glared at her. "I got a divorce. Happy?"

Alice gave her best sympathetic smile. "I'm so sorry."

"Don't be. Unless you slept with my ex-husband, which isn't out of the bounds of reality. Has anyone ever told you that you smile too much?"

Alice didn't know what to say to this. So she moved on to the next question. "Do you have any long term goals?"

"Getting you out of the house and finding Evie to give her a good slap."

"Evie?"

"You must have met her at the door. Tall, hot, rich-looking. Also, irritating, interfering, and irritating."

"You said irritating twice."

Vivien snorted. "I couldn't think of another 'I' word."

Alice put down the questionnaire. "She obviously cares about you," she said. "Evie, I mean. If she's the one that set you up with this."

"She cares. Sometimes a little too much. There's nothing wrong with me that time won't fix. She should stop pressing the issue."

"How long has it been since your divorce?" Alice asked.

"Almost a year."

A long time. Time enough that Vivien should be starting to move on at least a little. It was clear to Alice that this woman needed help. Not that she thought Foster Davison was going to be the right person to do that. But still. She cleared her throat.

"You think you need more time?"

Vivien's eyes scooted away, she looked at the wall, anything to avoid eye contact. "Yes."

Alice sighed and picked up the questionnaire again. This wasn't her business. She needed to get the questionnaire done and then get out of here. That was all.

The woman was brash, grumpy, irritable and couldn't even spare a smile. Not to mention that she was rude. Get the job done, get out, Alice told herself.

"What are your greatest fears?"

❊ ❊ ❊

"Heights," Viv said. "Oh, and bananas."

"Bananas?" the girl looked up in surprise.

Viv flashed her an evil grin. She couldn't help it. She was so sweet and innocent-looking, so trusting and naive. "They remind me of penises."

Alice flushed red and Viv sat back in satisfaction. This was completely ridiculous. She'd promised Evie she'd sit through the interview, but that was it. Once this girl was out of the house, she'd fulfilled her obligation.

"Um, do you have problems with organization and cleaning?"

Viv lifted an eyebrow.

The girl gulped. "I'll just mark 'yes' for that one, shall I?"

"What is a life coach, anyway?" Viv asked. Max was whimpering in his sleep and she wondered if she'd given him clean water in his bowl.

The girl flushed again and Viv asked herself how old she was. Slim, blonde, with the kind of pale skin that freckled in the sun, an oddly wide mouth. She couldn't be more than twenty or so.

"We teach people how to live," she said simply.

"Well, I hate people telling me what to do, so, you know, this probably isn't going to be a match made in heaven."

The girl rubbed at her nose. "Um, what about social support systems? Friends? Family in the area?"

"For god's sake," Viv snapped. "How the hell that's any of your damn business, I don't know. What is the point of all these questions?"

"To get a baseline?"

"You answered a question with a question. Exactly how experienced are you with this life coaching business?"

"I—"

Max growled then leaped up, barking and running at the window. Viv saw a shadow flitting past. "Goddammit," she yelled, jumping up. "Those goddamned kids need to stay on their own side of the damn lawn, how hard is that to understand?" She flung the window open. "Get off my property!"

But the kids were already gone. Viv slammed the window closed.

"Those kids were pretty small," the girl said.

What was her name? Alice, that was it. Like Alice in Wonderland. Just as damn curious too. Well, Viv for one had had enough. "Not your business," she snapped. "In fact, none of this is. I told Evie I'd do this, so what else do you need from me?"

She could see the blonde weighing up her options. "The form..." she began.

"Leave it here, I can read and write perfectly well. If I need to, I can fill it out."

"Okay." She slid the paper onto the coffee table where it joined a stack of old People magazines that Viv had found in the garage last summer.

"That it?" Viv said.

Alice nodded, silky blonde hair falling over her shoulder.

"Then why don't we both call this quits?" said Viv. "You know where the door is."

Alice got up. "Thank you for your time," she said politely.

"Stop damn well smiling so much," said Viv. "You'll break your face one day."

The smile dropped away as Alice slowly backed out of the room.

"Don't let the door hit you on the way out," Viv called after her.

She went back to the window. The kids were definitely gone. The front door creaked as it opened and then clicked closed. Finally. Alone. That was all she asked for, all she'd wanted. She hadn't asked to interrupt her day with unscheduled visits and bizarre life coaches.

She heard an engine start and mumbled some kind of prayer of thanks that Alice was driving away. Then she re-arranged the blankets on the couch so that they were more nest-like again.

Max whimpered and settled back down on the rug.

"Damn straight," Viv told him. "We've got plans today, you and I. And we're starting off with that Ted Bundy documentary that we've been meaning to watch."

Max opened one eye and closed it again as Viv grabbed the remote.

The life coaching questionnaire stirred in the draft as she wrapped herself in the blankets, then floated, unseen, to the ground.

CHAPTER SIX

There was no one to stop her, so Alice went home.

She was exhausted and frankly, the disastrous meeting she'd just had was only going to prove that she was not cut out for this job at all. Disney princess was looking like a better and better career choice.

She slid her key into the front door, turning it and pushing the door open, thinking only of kicking off her shoes and maybe treating herself to a glass of wine before starting that job search all over.

Which was about when she heard the sound of breaking glass coming from the kitchen.

Her heart leaped into her throat. She gritted her teeth and grabbed the first thing she could find in the hallway. Someone was in the apartment. Three in the afternoon and the place should be empty. Harrison was at work, there was no way anyone should be here.

Gripping the golf umbrella nice and tight she advanced toward the kitchen. She closed her eyes, said a quick prayer, then burst through the door with a yell, brandishing the umbrella.

"What the fuck?"

She stopped just before the umbrella would have hit Harrison's bent head. Her roommate was crouched over, picking up large pieces of glass from the kitchen floor.

"What are you doing here?" Alice asked, the umbrella heavy in her hand.

"I might ask you about the same question," said Harrison, standing up and dusting her hands over the trash can. "It's your first day. How on earth can you be home so early?"

Alice bit her lip. She wasn't one to be negative. But she couldn't lie either. "Um, maybe not the most successful first day?" she ventured.

Harrison grabbed two cups, the full coffee pot from the machine, and nodded toward a chair. "Sit and tell me all."

Alice sighed. Where to begin? "Well, Foster Davison is kind of an asshole, but it doesn't really matter since he's in the hospital right now."

Harrison frowned at her and poured the coffee. "Did you put him in the hospital?"

"Lord, no," Alice said, laughing. "He had some kind of attack or something at lunch. I've got no idea what it was." She should probably at least send some flowers. "And then he kind of threw me in at the deep end."

"In what way?" Harrison asked, sitting down and pushing a cup toward Alice.

"Well, he was supposed to be going to a client meeting and since he was being driven away in an ambulance I offered to cancel it. But he made me go instead."

"He made you an immediate life coach?"

"Kind of, I guess. And, well, I wasn't exactly great at it."

Harrison grinned. "You're great at everything, Al. Come on. How bad could it really have been?"

"Bad," Alice said, remembering Vivien's snarl and admonishment to smile less. "All I was supposed to do was go and ask questions to fill out a form. I didn't even get the thing half done before she threw me out."

"She?" Harrison asked, lifting an eyebrow. "So is she going to be wife number one? Are you planning the wedding yet?"

"I'm not that bad," Alice said.

"Yes, yes you are," said Harrison. "You plan weddings with every woman from the mail-lady to the girl at the deli on the corner. You practically had the two of us walking down the aisle."

Which Alice would have protested except she'd been struck by an odd thought. She wasn't quite as bad as Harrison was suggesting. But she did have a bad habit of imagining herself in relationships with most women she met.

Except Vivien.

Vivien Curtis was some kind of weird exception to the rule. Not that she wasn't a good-looking woman, she was. Yet the thought of fantasizing about her in any way, shape or form hadn't occurred to Alice in the slightest. Huh.

"Anyway, she threw me out. So even if I had been planning a wedding, I'm guessing it's off," Alice said. "She's probably not about to sign a contract with Foster either, which might be for the best. He's only interested in the money, not that he's making that much of it at the moment."

"I thought you said he was super good at what he does and famous and stuff?" Harrison said, fiddling with her cup.

Alice shrugged. "I guess he's coached everyone already and has run out of people who don't know what to do with their lives? Not that it matters. I don't think this is the job for me. I mean, I'm definitely organized enough to be an assistant. But this life coaching thing is kind of creepy, poking around in people's private business and all."

"Ah," said Harrison and she was staring deep into her coffee.

"What?" Alice asked.

"Nothing, nothing. I just... I thought maybe you'd found your thing, that's all," Harrison said. "Like your calling or whatever."

The kitchen clock ticked and there was the comforting smell of coffee. But something was wrong. Out of place. Alice couldn't quite decide what. Except the place really shouldn't smell of coffee if no one had been home all day.

"Why are you home?" she asked, realizing that Harrison hadn't answered the question the first time she'd asked.

Harrison just kept on staring into her coffee.

"Harrison."

"I don't want to lie to you, Al."

"Then don't!" Alice said. "Tell me the truth. What's wrong?"

Harrison closed her eyes and let out a breath. "I, uh, I've been laid off."

They hadn't known each other that long, but Alice knew that Harrison's job was important to her. She was a pharmaceutical rep, and she loved it. Not to mention the fact that she earned a fair amount of money. Enough that she'd helped Alice out with the rent a couple of times when Alice had been out of work.

"It's not your fault," Alice said, leaning forward and reaching out to take Harrison's hand.

"I know that. Just bad luck, I suppose."

Alice nodded. "When?" she asked.

"Pfff. Two weeks ago."

"Two weeks?" Alice asked in amazement. "But—"

"But I've been leaving the house every morning, I know," Harrison said looking shame-faced. "I thought I could find another job fast and you'd never know. No one would ever know. But no one's hiring and it's been harder than I thought. Today, with you being out at work for the first time, I thought I might just give myself one day off. One day not to search, not to be disappointed again. One day to feel sorry for myself and eat grilled cheese and watch soap operas."

Alice's heart about broke. Harrison was hurting, it was plain to see. "That sounds like an excellent plan," she said. "Why don't you go and find something suitably pulpy to watch and I'll get started on the grilled cheese?"

"Al, I don't want you to worry."

"Me? Worry? You're the one that has to stop worrying. You'll find something, Harrison. It might take a little longer than you'd like, but you will. You're right that this is bad luck. But the great thing about luck is that it can change."

Harrison cleared her throat. "Finances," she said.

"Another thing for you not to worry about," Alice said stoutly.

"But—"

"But nothing. You helped me out when I needed it and I fully intend to repay the favor. I can't believe you'd think any different of me."

At this Harrison finally smiled. "I wouldn't think any different of you, Al. You're the kindest, sweetest person in the world. But you can't carry the whole rent."

"Yes," Alice said, getting up. "Yes, I can."

"How?" pressed Harrison.

Alice shrugged. "I keep my job with Foster."

"But he's an asshole!"

"He's also in hospital for at least the foreseeable future," Alice pointed out. "And all I have to do is smile and play nice until you find a job then you can cover for me while I find something else. Easy, right? Then neither of us will owe anyone anything."

"Smile and play nice? Can you really do that?"

"I was born to do it," Alice said, grabbing sandwich bread from the cupboard. "Now weren't you going to go turn on the TV and start feeling sorry for yourself?"

Harrison got up and caught Alice's hand by the wrist before pulling her into a bear hug. "I don't think I've got the right to feel sorry for myself," she mumbled. "Not when I've got someone like you to watch my back."

"Oh, I don't know," Alice grinned. "You haven't tasted my grilled cheese yet. I make it with mayo, just like my mid-western mom taught me."

A look of horror passed over Harrison's face. "You are kidding, right?"

"Wait until you taste it," Alice said. "And you'll find out."

Harrison backed out of the kitchen making retching noises as Alice laughed and got cheese from the refrigerator. She didn't let the smile drop until Harrison was well out of sight.

She had to keep the job with Foster. Which was fine, she could make the sacrifice. But after the mess she'd made of the interview with Vivien Curtis, would Foster even consider keeping her on?

CHAPTER SEVEN

The sun was shining and it stung her eyes. Viv scowled and wished she'd brought her sunglasses. The spikes of lights weren't doing much to improve her morning.

"Come on, Max." She pulled at the leash, but the dog seemed more interested in eating grass than peeing. Grass that he'd barf up on the carpet, no doubt. "For fuck's sake."

Suddenly, Max scented something, and pulled at the leash. Finally. She practically jogged after him. Exercise wasn't top of her list when it came to priorities, but getting home and safe again was, so she let herself puff and pant until her legs nearly gave out.

She was on the verge of collapse when she smelled coffee. Thank all the gods. "Max! Stop!"

For once, he listened, snuffling at her head gently as she tied him up to a bike rack outside of the coffee shop. She ruffled his fur. "I'll bring you a cookie," she promised.

Then she took a deep breath and barged into the shop.

It was all sanded wood and bare walls, hipster-ish and not at all her scene. Though truth be told, Viv couldn't remember the last time she'd been in a coffee shop. She marched up to the counter. Best to get this over with.

Opening the cupboard to an empty coffee jar this morning had done nothing to improve her mood. And since groceries weren't being delivered until the afternoon, this was her chance to get precious caffeine.

"Latte," she said. "And throw in one of those oatmeal cookies too."

"Good morning, ma'am," smiled the girl behind the counter.

Viv steeled herself. "Good morning," she managed to say. "A latte and an oatmeal cookie."

The girl stared at her.

"Please," Viv added.

The girl smiled and rang up the order. "That'll be seven eighty, please. What's your name, ma'am?"

"None of your damn business," barked Viv, hackles rising. Instinctively, she looked down and saw the name-badge pinned onto the girl's apron. Alice. Which made her even more irritated, like the figment of that stupid life coach was following her around or something.

"I need to know what name to put on the order," explained the girl, patiently.

Ostentatiously, Viv looked over her left shoulder, then her right, surveying the empty store. "Because?"

The girl huffed. "More customers might come in after I take your order," she pointed out.

And Viv's already slim patience disappeared down a crack in the distressed hard-wood floor. "Give me my caffeine."

The girl eyed her for a moment, then apparently decided that this was not a fight worth having and began to make the order. Viv relaxed a little.

Alice. What were the chances? Though maybe it was one of those old fashioned names that had become cool again. Not a bad name, actually. In fact, she quite liked the feel of it in her mouth, the roundness of that A, the softness of the C.

Maybe she'd been hard on the girl. Both girls. Both Alices. Maybe Evie was kind of onto something. Not that she needed a life coach, far from it. If anyone knew how to live life it was Vivien Curtis.

Vivien Curtis who'd had hair of all the colors of the rainbow, who'd run away to Costa Rica for three months her sophomore year of college, who'd partied and danced and seen the world. No, Vivien Curtis didn't need lessons in life.

On the other hand, maybe this was all... getting out of hand. Almost a year was a long time. Evie had the right to want her old friend back. Viv felt a pang of pain in her heart. She had a right to want her old self back.

It was just that it seemed so far to travel back now. So far from what she'd become to what she'd been.

"Here you go, ma'am," chirped coffee-Alice.

Viv experimented with a smile which made the girl visibly flinch, then sighed and took her coffee and Max's cookie.

THE CAR WAS parked in the driveway, bumper to bumper with Viv's SUV. Max barked when he saw it and Viv squinted then groaned as Evie climbed out of the front seat.

"Accosting me in front of my own house isn't the same as calling before you visit."

"I just happened to be in the area," Evie said airily.

"Bullshit."

"Fine. I wanted to know how it went yesterday with the life coach. Since you won't answer any of my messages..."

Viv patted her pockets then swore. "No idea where my mobile is, sorry."

"Again? Probably down one of the couch cushions. Come on. I'll help you look for it."

Evie plucked the house keys out of Viv's hand and strode toward the house. By the time Viv was inside and had released Max from his leash, she was already banging around in the kitchen.

"No coffee?" she shouted through.

"All out," Viv answered. She had a feeling that this wasn't going to be the easiest conversation. Once Evie had her mind set on something, persuading her otherwise was a nightmare. And Evie seemed very taken with the idea of a life coach.

"Tea it is then."

Viv rolled her eyes and kicked off her shoes before joining Evie in the kitchen. Best to go in on the offensive.

"I don't want a life coach." There. Said.

"Why on earth not?" Evie said, moving aside tea boxes in the cupboard. "Was he horrific?"

Viv ignored the question and the pronoun. "I don't want someone poking around in my life," she said pointedly, as Evie opened the next cupboard and began shuffling through herbal teas.

Finally, Evie turned back. "Viv, I love you. Always have, always will. But this needs to end. You need to accept that maybe you could use a little help."

"I don't need help. You're making me sound like I'm crazy or something."

Evie arched an eyebrow.

"What?"

"You're practically a recluse, you leave the house only to walk the dog. You're grumpy and snappy and a bear to everyone. You have no friends, and your house is slowly turning into a hoarder's wet dream."

Viv opened her mouth, closed it, then opened it again. "Don't pull any punches then."

Evie sighed. "Viv, I've tried to help you. I've invited you out, I've been here for you every step of the way. I know that this has been hard, I know that you've suffered. But I don't want you to end up as some angry old lady who throws rocks at kids from her porch."

"Huh, I hadn't thought of doing that."

"Not the time for joking, Viv. I'm being serious. I'm your best friend, and it's my job to tell you the uncomfortable truths of life. I don't like it any more than you do."

Viv bit her lip and shrugged. Maybe Evie had a point. Hadn't she just been thinking pretty much the same thing herself? "Okay, fine, maybe I could use a little help. But a life coach? Seriously, Eve?"

Evie looked down at the ground and scratched her nose in the exact same way that she had two decades ago when Viv's father had asked her if she'd broken the garage window.

"Spill it," Viv said immediately. "Whatever it is that you're holding back, spit it out."

A short pause, then Evie muttered: "I can go to London."

Viv frowned and then understood. "The job? You got it?"

Evie nodded, still not looking her in the eye.

"But... but that's amazing. That's the dream. Six months in London, come on, Evie, I'm so proud of you." Because she was, even if the thought of being without Evie for six months made her feel a little sick.

Evie sighed. "I can't take it, Viv."

"Why on earth not?"

And now she did look up and her dark eyes were fierce. "Because I can't leave you, not like this."

Suddenly, the pieces all clicked together. "Which is why you arranged for the life coach. To be my babysitter."

"Not exactly. I thought this might be a good opportunity for you too. You'll get a little help to get your life back on track, I'll know that someone's keeping an eye on you, and I'll get to come back to my old best friend."

"Jesus, Evie. I'll be fine, I'm not going to hurt myself or anything else, I swear."

"I don't want to come back to find you buried under a pile of out-dated newspapers, or to find that the kids next door have snapped and stuffed Tickle-Me-Elmo in the exhaust of your car."

"Just go. I'll be fine."

"No." Evie crossed her arms. "I'm not going unless I know that you're in good hands. And that you're trying to make things better."

And Viv felt her will melting. She didn't want this. She didn't need a babysitter. She especially didn't need that interfering little Alice in Wonderland poking around her life and smiling all the damn time.

But Evie had been there for her during all the dark nights and the darker mornings. Evie had been her life-line when she hadn't even known she'd needed one. And this job was Evie's dream.

"A fucking life coach, are you for real?" she said, looking at Evie's truculent face.

Then Evie grinned and Viv knew that the fight was lost.

CHAPTER EIGHT

The hospital smelled like... hospital. Detergent and bleach and stuff that Alice really didn't want to think about. She clutched the flowers tight in her hand and waited her turn at the reception desk.

The receptionist was a red-head, bright and cheerful and Alice could picture her working in the garden, standing up to brush soil off her knees before she came in for a hot cup of tea. She smiled a little at the thought of calling out to her to wipe her feet before she came in.

Then she started wondering what her name was and was so busy doing that that she almost missed her turn.

"Next?"

The man behind her elbowed her between the shoulder-blades and Alice stumbled forward, blushing already.

"I, uh, hello."

"Hi," smiled the red-head. "Can I help you?"

"Hospital," spat out Alice. Yes, well done there. She was obviously coming across as someone who needed a mental ward more than wherever it was Foster had been taken.

"Yes," said the re-head slowly. "This is the hospital. Are you lost? Do you speak English?"

Alice blushed even more furiously and seriously considered faking a French accent for a second but dismissed the idea since she'd never actually been to France. She cleared her throat. "Um, sorry, my brain zapped for a second there."

The woman laughed. "Not a problem. Who are you looking for?"

Her smile was wide, her laugh musical, and Alice could see herself falling in love with someone like this. Someone bright and smiling and loving. Someone generous and giving. Someone who was waiting very patiently for her to answer a question. Crap.

"Uh, Foster Davison?"

The red-head clacked on some computer keys then gave very precise instructions that Alice tried very hard to listen to, but then ended up staring into green eyes. Which meant that five minutes later she was stumbling into the staff cafeteria, no closer to finding Foster than when she started.

It could be for the best, she thought. What Foster didn't know couldn't hurt him. She needed the job and she hadn't been fired yet. Once Foster knew she'd screwed up with Vivien Curtis then she might be out of work.

Plus, maybe he'd be in a better frame of mind once he'd recovered from... whatever it was he had.

"Help you?"

A tall young man in a white coat stopped her wandering blindly around the hallways and eventually led her to a ward made up of four beds. Foster was reclining in the one closest to the door, pale and sweaty looking.

Alice took a deep breath. Here went nothing.

She felt sorry for the man. He was alone. Maybe his family, girlfriend, husband, whatever, had already visited, she told herself. But she had a feeling that wasn't true. She had a feeling that Foster Davison was more alone than he'd like people to know.

Still clutching the now slightly wilted flowers she walked to the end of his bed.

"What now?" he snapped, then opened one eye to see Alice. "Oh, it's you."

"I, um, brought these?" she said, holding out the flowers.

His hair was messed up, the widow's peak not so prominent now that it wasn't all sleeked back. He stared at the flowers for a moment.

"I could give them to a nurse to deal with?" Alice said finally.

He looked almost relieved. "Yes, do that."

Alice looked around, noting that Foster had an IV, that the curtains around his bed were open, unlike the other cubicles in the room, and that there were no visitor chairs by his bed at all.

"So, um..." she started.

"You saw the client?" he interrupted.

"Yes," said Alice. "But more importantly, how are you feeling?"

"Like hell," he said, and she believed it. "I've got the gall bladder of an eighty year old woman, apparently. It hurts and they're wheeling away to cut me open any minute now, so why don't we get to the point, Anna."

"Alice," Alice interjected.

"Whatever. The client meeting."

Alice sighed, itching to run away and really wishing she hadn't come. "It, uh, didn't maybe go so well?" she ventured.

Foster struggled to sit up in bed, then was pulled back by his IV and almost growled, though whether in pain or irritation she couldn't tell. "Did you fuck this up?"

"No, it wasn't like that—"

"Don't tell me what it was like or not like," he snapped. Color was starting to bloom in his cheeks. "We do not lose this client, do you understand? You do not lose this client."

"I—"

"You nothing. This is the first new client I've had in two months now and I'm damned if you're fucking this up for me, Angie. You get your shit together and you keep this contract. It's an open deal, no limit on spending, we can go on as long as we want. I need this client. I—" He broke off with a grimace of pain.

"It's Alice," Alice said again. She'd been right, Foster Davison was nowhere near as successful as he wanted others to believe. "And what exactly do you want me to do? The client isn't interested in having a life coach."

"Then make her see the virtues of having someone tell her how to be happy," he barked. "Nobody thinks that they want someone telling them what to do, but in the end, we all want it. We all want to pass along the responsibilities of life to someone else for a while. Just show her what the experience is like, make her believe."

Alice tapped the flowers on the rail at the end of his bed. "Even if I could persuade her, what then?" she asked. "You're about to have major surgery."

"Then you'll step in. I hired you for a reason."

"To be your assistant."

"Then damn well assist me in keeping this client!" He was almost yelling now.

She almost rolled her eyes and then remembered that there was rent to pay and stopped herself. "How exactly do you want me to do that?" she asked, which seemed reasonable enough. "I'm not a life coach, remember?"

He snorted. "You think I am? I was a psych major at a third rate community college. Life coach is a title, nothing more. Go online, find some stuff out. Go with your gut. Read people, see what makes them tick, push them in the direction of what makes them happy."

Alice frowned. "You're saying I should make things up as I go along?"

Another snort. "Like I do. It's not exactly hard. These people don't have serious mental issues, I check that out beforehand. They're just looking for someone to take the responsibilities away for a while. They're looking for someone to make decisions for them for a few weeks until they can see a clear path. That's all." He scowled at her. "Are you decisive?"

"I guess," said Alice, still trying to take all this in.

"Yeah, that answer inspires confidence." He winced in pain again.

"Look, I can't do this," Alice began.

"Then you're fired," said Foster.

"No, wait..."

"Are you Mr. Davison's next of kin?" A blonde nurse in scrubs had appeared from somewhere.

"No!" both Alice and Foster said at once.

"Well, okay then," said the nurse, backing off a step. "Mr. Davison, it's about time to get you up to pre-op."

Foster turned to Alice. "I don't know how to make this any clearer, Amy," he said. "You land the client and keep her on until I'm ready to take over, or you're fired, it's really that simple."

"But—" Alice said.

"But nothing. I'm about to have a life-threatening operation!" Foster practically screamed.

"Actually, it's a fairly standard procedure," said the nurse.

They both ignored her.

"So what's it to be?" Foster said.

He was desperate, Alice could see that. The problem was, so was she. She went over the options in her head. But there weren't exactly many of them. She needed the money, she needed the job, Foster needed her to get Vivien on board.

The nurse was already hooking Foster's IV bag onto the bed, preparing him to move. Alice swallowed. She wasn't at all sure she could do this. She also wasn't at all sure that Vivien Curtis would ever agree to life coaching.

But she owed Harrison.

She took a deep breath, then nodded. "Fine, I'll do it."

Foster collapsed back onto the bed. "Thank fuck. String her along for a couple of days, Ari, I'll be back before you know it."

"It's going to be more than a couple of days," the nurse said, taking the brake off Foster's hospital bed.

And Alice watched her wheel Foster away wondering just what she was thinking by agreeing to this.

"My name's Alice," she said softly, before realizing that she was still holding the bunch of flowers.

45

CHAPTER NINE

When Viv opened the door to a sea of balloons and a bouquet so large she couldn't see who was behind it, her first instinct was to slam the door closed.

She was already in the middle of doing so when a voice came from behind the flowers.

"Can we talk?"

The voice was vaguely familiar, but to be honest, she had better things to do than solve mysteries, and the balloons were making her feel vaguely uncomfortable in a way she didn't quite understand, bobbing out there like tiny buoys.

"No," she said firmly, and was about to slam the door again.

"Please?" the flowers moved and a small, pale face appeared. Alice's hair was pulled back and she looked all of twelve years old.

Viv sighed. Crap.

She'd promised Evie in the end, of course she had. How could she possibly sabotage her best friend's dream opportunity? And Evie was the one paying for the stupid life coach, after all. All Viv had to do was show up. Or be showed up to. Or however the hell this was supposed to work.

Having said life coach appear unannounced, breaking her rule about visiting without calling as well as a brand-new rule about no ridiculous amounts of balloons in her house, was an unexpected turn of events.

"About what?" she said, playing for time since there really was only one thing that Alice could possibly want to talk to her about.

"Um, about life coaching?" Alice said. Her eyes were blue and pleading and really, she looked like a girl scout selling cookies.

Except that Viv would actually want to buy girl scout cookies.

Still, she'd promised Evie. And maybe it was easier this way. She hadn't exactly come up with a plan for how she was going to call the girl and ask her to come back. Apologizing wasn't her style. But then, neither was life coaching.

She sighed and stood back, opening the front door wide. "Oh no," she said, as Alice started to push her balloons and flowers through the doorway. "Those stay outside."

"They'll float away," Alice said doubtfully.

"Then put them in your car."

"You'll keep the door open?" Alice narrowed her eyes in suspicion.

Viv nodded and held the door wide as Alice struggled to fit all the balloons back into the back seat of her car.

"I'm not seven," she said, when Alice came back to the door, breathless and flushed. "And it's not my birthday."

"Balloons make some people happy," Alice said.

"Not me."

"Noted," said Alice. "What about flowers?"

"No feelings either way, really."

"Good," Alice said, finally stepping into the house and depositing the bouquet in its vase on the hallway table. "I'm not sure I could fit these back in the car again anyway."

"If you're trying to bribe me into accepting your services, you should try chocolate, or at least something food based," Viv said, closing the door. "I'm not exactly a balloons and flowers kind of girl."

Alice shrugged. "Listen, this process is all about making you happy, finding your happiness. It was worth a shot, so I took it. You could have been charmed."

"You could have been killed driving with all that in your back seat," Viv pointed out. Against her will she was kind of starting to... well, not like Alice exactly. But appreciate her a little more, maybe. She had balls showing up again like this, and obviously she wasn't afraid of taking risks.

"I wasn't," said Alice. "And do you think we could talk, please? I'd like another shot at convincing you to go along with our process. I think maybe we got off on the wrong foot."

Viv sensed an opportunity here.

After all, Alice didn't know what she'd promised Evie. Or she assumed she didn't. Which meant that there could be some room for negotiation here, some way to make this whole life coaching thing a little less onerous and invasive than it might otherwise be.

She sniffed. "I suppose you can have another go. There's no harm in trying, is there?" she said, leading Alice into the living room. "I'm not promising anything though."

"I wouldn't dream of assuming that you were," said Alice, depositing herself back on the couch in the exact position she'd been in the day before.

Viv sat down and crossed her legs, ignoring the hole in the knee of her sweatpants. "Go on then," she said. "Convince me."

❊ ❊ ❊

Yes, she'd panicked. Turning up at the door with balloons and flowers hadn't been the smoothest move. She'd just thought that maybe she'd make an impact. And whose heart wouldn't be softened by balloons and flowers?

Well, Vivien Curtis's apparently. But most other people would love it, wouldn't they? Besides, she'd put it all on the corporate credit card that she'd found on Foster's desk. She was supposed to do everything she could to land the client, right?

"Well, um, here's the thing," she said. "I think you need some help."

"And why's that?" Viv arched an eyebrow.

Alice looked around at the cluttered living room. "Because it's kind of obvious. Are you happy, Vivien?"

"It's Viv. And, well, yes. I suppose. I don't know. I'm an adult. Adults aren't meant to be happy, are they? We're all too busy paying taxes and cleaning toilets."

In that small moment, Alice suddenly settled into what she was doing. No, she wasn't trained. But Viv's words had hurt her. Who thought that adults couldn't be happy? Viv needed help. Maybe Foster was onto something here. Maybe making Viv happy wasn't such a terrible thing to be doing. Assuming Viv would agree.

"I'm pretty happy," Alice said. "Not every second, but most of the time."

Viv rolled her eyes. "Then aren't you special."

Alice sat forward. "What's so terrible about this?" she asked. "Your friend wants you to be happy. I would like to help you be happy. You're obviously unhappy. What about all that sounds so awful to you?"

"Oh, I don't know. A stranger poking through my life? Prying? Telling me what to do?"

"I won't pry," Alice said immediately. "I'm not interested in learning your secrets. I'm interested in helping you have a more fulfilling and contented life. That's it. And yes, maybe sometimes I'll give you direction, but it's not like I can force you to do anything."

Viv sniffed again.

And Alice took a chance. She was observant. She'd seen the framed photographs in the hall, she could tell that the house had originally been decorated with care. "You were happy once, Viv. How about we get you back to a place where you can feel that way again?"

"How exactly is that supposed to work?"

Was it just her, or was Viv starting to bend? Alice took a breath. "Well, um, I guess we try a few different things and find out what makes you happy and then we clear some of the chaos out of your life so that you have more time for the things that make you happy. We, um, confront your fears too," she added because she definitely remembered Foster mentioning that one.

"Huh," was all Viv said.

Alice crossed her fingers. "So what do you say?"

"You don't stay at my house," said Viv. "I get to have my own space and private time."

"Obviously."

"And if I tell you we're not doing something or talking about something, then you'll let it go?"

"Of course."

She was holding her breath now. She had more. She had statistics she'd found online about happiness. She was prepared to pull out the 'do it for your worried friend' card. But she sensed that maybe, just maybe, Viv wasn't quite as gruff as she'd have Alice believe.

"Alright then."

"What?" Alice said. "Really?"

"I'm not paying for it," Viv said. "What do I care?"

"Oh, great," said Alice. Quickly, she opened up the folder she'd brought from the car. She'd found the contracts on Foster's computer and printed one out, along with an NDA that she'd sign herself in front of Viv. "If you can just sign here then," she said, pushing the document over to Viv.

She waited as Viv scrawled her name, unable to believe her luck. In truth, this had all been a last, desperate attempt. She hadn't really believed that Viv would ever agree, she'd seemed so definite the day before. At the very least she'd expected a lot more of a fight.

But it looked like Viv was willing to play along after all.

"So," Viv said, sliding the contract back and sitting back in her chair. "Where do we start then?"

Alice opened her mouth then slammed it shut.

She'd been so sure that Viv wasn't going to agree that she hadn't thought this far ahead...

CHAPTER TEN

E vie clasped her into a hug and Viv let it happen. And once it was happening, it felt so soft and warm and beautiful that for an instant she wanted to stay in Evie's arms for the rest of her life. She pulled back hurriedly.

"Behave yourself," she said, already missing the feel of human contact.

It had been so long since someone had held her. So long since someone had touched her. She actively avoided being touched most of the time, if she was being honest. So long that she'd forgotten how nice it could feel.

"I'm not the one we're worrying about here," Evie said with a grin. "I'm a damn sight more worried about you behaving yourself. Think you've got a handle on all this?"

"I've got it covered. I said I'd do the life coaching, so I'll do it," said Viv. "Not that I'm happy about it."

"You might be when you start to see some results," Evie said. "By the time I get back here, you could be a whole different person."

"There's nothing wrong with who I am now."

"Yeah, except you're a grumpy hermit who scares away children."

"Aren't you supposed to be on a plane?"

"Okay, okay," said Evie. "I'm getting out of your hair. You'll miss me when I'm gone though."

A spike went through Viv's stomach. She was already missing Evie, and she hadn't even left yet.

Evie reached out and took both her hands. "You're going to call me if you need me, right, Viv?"

Viv nodded.

"And it's only six months. I'll be back. I'm still here for you, Viv. Just on a different continent is all."

"So I might get some peace and quiet for a change."

"Be grumpy all you like, but I'm going to miss you and I know you'll miss me. You're going to really work at this, Viv, aren't you? You promised me. I want you to be happy again and I don't know how else to help you."

Viv swallowed. "I'll try," she promised. She wanted some of her old self back too. If only because it meant that people might stop trying to interfere with her life.

Evie clasped her into one last hug and Viv clung on for dear life until Evie had to pull away or risk missing her flight.

"Catch you on the flip-side," Evie said, just like she had when they were kids.

Viv gave her an oddly watery smile as she turned and waved before getting into her car. She couldn't remember the last time that Evie hadn't been on the periphery of her life, orbiting and stabilizing her.

Yeah, the astronomy of that comparison probably didn't work. Still though, there was a gaping hole where Evie was supposed to fit. And she wasn't about to let some damn life coach fill that hole. No, it would remain safely Evie shaped until Evie came home.

She slammed the door and Max started barking.

"Oh, hush," she told him. "She'll be home before you know it." She trailed him into the kitchen and opened the treat jar. "In the meantime, you'd better prepare yourself for the invasion of Little Miss Sunshine."

Max whined until she handed over a treat.

SUN STREAMED THROUGH the living room window and caught on Alice's hair, making it look gold rather than plain blonde.

"Well then," Viv said gruffly, crossing her arms. "Where do we start?"

Alice opened up the bag she was carrying and emptied it onto the couch. Rolls of trash bags bounced off the cushions and clunked onto the floor.

"With cleaning," said Viv, staring at the bags.

"With tidying," Alice corrected. "A tidy environment helps you think more clearly. Believe it or not, there are plenty of studies on the subject. I've got print-outs if you want to see them?"

"God no," said Viv, still looking at the trash bags. Cleaning was bad enough without having to read a scientific analysis of it.

"A little at a time is the trick to handling seemingly overwhelming situations," said Alice and Viv sort of wanted to slap her.

"I'm not a child. I understand how cleaning, sorry, tidying works," she said. "And if we're going to do it, I suppose we should get started."

"I want you to take a bag and just put in the things that can be thrown away. I want you to think about if the object is something you have used recently, or if it's something you will use. If not, it goes in the bag. We're de-cluttering," Alice said, tearing off a bag. "And we can start right here in the living room."

Max whined and got up from under the coffee table before lazily walking off into the kitchen. Viv jealously watched him go. "Fine. Let's get on with it then."

She took a bag and started with the magazines on the table. It wasn't that she thought they were useful, or that she'd deliberately collected them, more that she never thought to throw them out. There never seemed much point. Throw them in the trash and she'd just have to take the trash out sooner.

Of course, now she had Alice to help take out the trash.

"How long were you married?"

The question took her by surprise. "Seven years."

"That's a long time."

"It's a long time when you find out that your asshole of an ex was cheating on you the entire time," said Viv, sliding a handful of take-out menus into her bag.

"That must have hurt," Alice said. She was picking up blankets from the couch and folding them neatly.

Hurt didn't cover it. Hurt was just a word. It did nothing to explain the raw, aching pain she'd felt when she'd found out. Bill had been forever. She'd found her person. And then all of a sudden that person wasn't who she'd thought he was and the world had tilted on its axis.

Somehow, the planet had never quite got back into alignment.

"It's a stupid institution anyway," Viv said, grabbing yet more magazines. "Tying yourself to someone for life, what an idiotic idea."

"I don't think so," Alice said. She skirted around the back of the couch so she could get the blankets on the other side. "One bad experience shouldn't ruin the entire institution. Marriage can be beautiful."

"Right," said Viv, sliding a paper plate with chip crumbs into the bag. "Like you'd know a thing about it. You're all of twelve."

"I'm twenty five," Alice said. "And you shouldn't give up on love just because some idiot couldn't see what he had."

It happened so fast that Viv wasn't sure how it had happened. She stepped back and turned at the exact time as Alice was moving and then Alice tripped and was falling and Viv was catching her by the elbows.

"Steady on there," Viv said.

Her hands were on Alice's arms and Alice's wide blue eyes were staring up at her and there was no way she was twenty five. Carefully, Viv let go. Carefully because, just like with Evie, it was becoming clear to her that she was missing contact. Missing holding, being held.

Not that holding Alice was an option.

Alice grinned. "Thanks, I can be clumsy."

"As well as a romantic," Viv said. "Marriage is for chumps, you'll find out soon enough if you haven't already." She stopped and eyed Alice. "You're not married, are you?"

"Nope," said Alice.

"Well, trust me, don't fall for it. You're better off alone. At least that way you get to decide what to watch on TV every night."

Alice ignored that. "This place is looking better already," she said, smiling.

Viv looked around and actually, Alice wasn't wrong. The living room did look brighter, nicer, with the blankets folded on the couch and the trash picked up, the coffee table clear for once.

"How about we move on to the kitchen?" Alice asked brightly.

"This whole life coaching thing isn't just about cleaning, is it?" Viv grumbled as she lugged her trash bag through to the kitchen.

"We're tidying," said Alice. "Not cleaning. We might run the vacuum around a little later, let's see how much we can get done in the next couple of hours."

Viv sighed. "This whole life coaching thing isn't just about *tidying*, is it?"

"Oh no," said Alice, sounding far too innocent. "Not at all."

"You sure about that?" prodded Viv.

Alice tossed her blonde hair back over her shoulders and grinned. "Absolutely sure. Tomorrow, for example, we won't be cleaning or tidying."

"We won't?" Viv asked suspiciously.

"Nope."

"What will we be doing then?"

Alice beamed and Viv found that the corners of her mouth were twitching slightly. Alice's happiness was somewhat contagious. When it wasn't irritating.

"It's a surprise," is all Alice would say.

CHAPTER ELEVEN

Harrison screwed up her nose. "I don't know, Al. Foster sounds like kind of an asshole."

"An asshole that's going to be paying our rent," Alice reminded her, drinking scalding coffee.

"I hate the idea of you working for someone you don't like, of you doing something you don't want to do," said Harrison. She was in sweats, her hair tied up.

Alice shrugged. "I'm not a fan of Foster, but the guy needs help. It looks like he's all alone in the world."

"Probably because he's the kind of asshole that doesn't remember anyone's name," Harrison snorted.

"But I'm not saying I'm hating this," said Alice. "Actually, it's going okay, I think. I like the idea of it, helping people find happiness, that's a good thing, right?"

"And what about this Viv person?"

Alice shrugged. "She's gruff, grumpy, but I think her bark's worse than her bite. She agreed to coaching, God knows why since she was so against the idea at first. But she does need the help."

Harrison sighed. "Are you falling for her, Al?"

"What?" Alice almost choked on her coffee. Her and Viv? Seriously? "Um, no. She's a client. In fact, she's probably the only woman in a fifty mile radius that I haven't imagined myself married to. Which is just as well since I'm pretty sure she wants to outlaw marriage just on principle."

Harrison poured cereal into a bowl. "I know you're doing this for me, and I do appreciate it. I've got an interview this afternoon. If I get the job, you can always quit yours."

"Don't count your chickens," Alice said, putting her cup down. "Besides, like I said, I'm not against the idea right now. Foster's going to be in recovery for ages, so it's not like I've got to deal with him on a daily basis. And Viv is... she's hurting. But I think underneath, she's probably a very nice person."

Harrison grunted at that. "Ever the optimist. What's on the schedule for today?"

"Fear-facing," Alice said. She'd read a whole thing about it on the internet a couple of days ago. This was one thing that was concrete, one thing she could actually plan. So she'd gone all out. She knew Foster did fear-facing, so maybe this was going to impress him. Maybe he'd write her a decent recommendation when she finally quit.

"Fear-facing," said Harrison. "Which means doing what exactly?"

Alice told her.

"Jesus Christ," was all Harrison said, shaking her head.

TWO AND A half hours later, Alice was thinking something very similar. Different words, much ruder ones, but the same kind of sentiment.

She glanced over at Viv who was pale as a sheet. Her dark hair was ruffling in the wind and a harness fit snugly around her body.

"I swear to all the gods," Viv said, teeth clenched. "If I ever get down from here, I will do serious damage to you, Little Miss Sunshine."

Alice gulped, not at all out of fear that Viv would actually do anything. There were far more pressing matters to be dealt with first.

"It's simple," the instructor was saying from behind them.

"You go to the edge, you step off. That's it. You can look or not look, up to you. All you really got to do is jump."

Alice squeezed her eyes tight shut. Not looking was the only option. "And you're sure this is safe?"

"Safe as houses. I checked all your gear myself," the guy said.

Instructor was over-stating things. He was a tattooed guy with no shirt on and dreads, all of about eighteen, chewing gum and leaning casually against the side of the metal platform. Almost as if there wasn't a two hundred and fifty foot drop behind him.

Alice whimpered. She heard herself doing it. What had she done?

"Hey!"

She opened her eyes a touch to see that Viv had shuffled closer. "Yes?"

"What the hell? This was all your idea. You were the one giving the lecture about facing my fears. And now you're up here shaking like a leaf and you can't even look over the side?"

"I, uh, I might not have thought this all the way through," Alice said.

Which was absolutely true. She hadn't thought any further ahead than the fact that Viv was afraid of heights and that the carnival in the city park had a bungee jump ride. She'd planned ahead, booked tickets, and been pleased with herself that she had a plan.

She hadn't considered the fact that a crane was going to winch them up two hundred and fifty feet into the sky. She definitely hadn't considered the fact that she too would be jumping. Only once they were up there had she realized that there was no way she could make a scared client jump alone.

"No shit," Viv said.

"Are you two jumping or not?" said the guy from behind them. "There's people waiting."

"Shut up," Viv said to him. She turned back to Alice. "We've got to get down from here, just close your eyes and step off the edge. It'll be over before you know it."

"I can't," Alice said, aware just in that moment that she absolutely couldn't. "I can't jump, Viv."

"I'm gonna need you guys to go in the next thirty seconds," said the guy.

Viv swore under her breath and Alice's breath was coming harder, her heart pounding. She opened her eyes enough so that she could see Viv's face. "I can't do this," she whispered.

Viv shot a look over the edge and visibly paled.

"Ten," drawled the guy behind them. "Nine."

"Fuck," Viv said.

Alice just looked at her pleadingly.

"Eight," said the guy. "Come on, or I'll push you."

Alice wailed.

"For fuck's sake," said Viv.

Then she was coming closer and Alice could feel her warmth, could feel that Viv was taking her in her arms, was holding her tight. Something changed inside her. The coldness of fear was replaced by comfort. She wrapped her arms around Viv, closing her eyes, burying her face in Viv's shirt.

"Life coaching is the worst—" began Viv.

But Alice didn't hear the rest because all of a sudden she was flying. Viv had held her and jumped, sending them both hurtling down to the ground. Not that Alice could see. Her face was still pushed into Viv's shirt, she was still enclosed in Viv's arms, she was still safe and almost calm.

Then the elastic stretched and snatched them back up again and Viv was laughing and Alice held her even closer, drinking in a smell of coconut and citrus.

"Woo-hoo," yelled out Viv as they bounced around. Then the crane was slowly lowering them back down to the ground and their harnesses were being unbuckled and Alice had to let go of Viv.

"That was fucking amazing," Viv said, her face flushed and her eyes bright. "I gotta say, Alice, you could be onto something here."

"You... you liked it?" Alice asked. Her stomach was stuck

somewhere in her throat and her knees weren't working.

"Liked it? It was incredible," Viv said. She was grinning wide and bright and Alice realized it was the first time she'd seen Viv really smile.

"I'm glad," she said, and she was. The fear was draining away, the shaking was stopping, and she was starting to feel warm and fuzzy inside. She'd helped. Viv was smiling. She grinned back.

"I think we need to talk about this," Viv said. "Come on, I'll buy you a frozen yogurt."

From satisfaction to... something else. Alice frowned, she'd thought Viv was happy, she thought she'd done well. "But—"

"Nope, no talking without fro-yo."

It wasn't until they both had pots in hands that Viv would talk.

"I'm gonna be honest and say I was doubtful about this whole life coaching thing," Viv said. "And I haven't particularly changed my mind. Yeah, you did good here, but one bungee jump isn't life changing. Nor, for that matter, is you scaring the hell out of yourself."

Alice blew out a breath. "Yeah, it was pretty unprofessional."

Viv actually laughed. "It was sort of funny though. I mean, you should have seen your face. Had you honestly not considered the fact that you'd be jumping too?"

Alice shook her head.

"Look, I'm here for the ride," Viv said. "For better or worse, I'm involved in this process now. But I think we need to start a little smaller. For both of our sakes."

"Right," Alice said.

"No more blindfolding me and forcing me out of the house."

Alice blushed.

"No more making me jump off tall objects whilst holding you like a frightened rabbit."

"Right."

"Maybe something a little more... practical."

Alice nodded. "More practical, got it."

Viv held out a hand. "In return, I'll try to be a little more open to your ideas. After all, this one turned out to be kind of fun. Shake on it."

Alice clasped her cold hand and shook. Smaller, more practical. She could do that. But in the back of her mind she could still see Viv's smile, could still feel Viv's arms around her, and she couldn't help but feel a little proud.

CHAPTER TWELVE

Max snuffled along the sidewalk, tail wagging at an amazing rate. The leash hung loose in Viv's hand as she followed him.

Last night, for the first time in so long she couldn't remember, she'd slept through the night.

It was an odd feeling, being well-rested. Sort of like being drunk, or being a kid, full of energy. It was different and Viv wasn't at all sure she approved of it.

She put the good night of sleep down to the fact that she'd used every shred of energy she'd had the day before getting herself and Alice down from that damn contraption at the carnival. The thought of it made her grin to herself.

Truthfully, it had been pretty awesome. She could still feel the way the wind had blown against her skin, the way her stomach had floated inside her, the way Alice had clung to her for dear life.

She sighed and checked her watch. She had a solid hour and a half before Alice was due to appear. God knows what the woman had planned for today. She might have promised to go small, but Viv wasn't convinced. Actually, she was starting to wonder just how much experience Alice had with life coaching.

Which was kind of ridiculous because Evie only ever dealt with the best in everything.

The thought of Evie made her feel heavier again. She missed

her. She actually missed the fact that there was no one to walk into her house uninvited. How dumb was that?

"Come on," she said to Max. "Let's get home."

If they walked fast, she could still have a little couch and Discovery Channel time before Alice appeared. A little time for herself. She liked the warm feeling that thought gave her inside, the comforting feeling. It felt very similar to how it had felt holding on to Alice yesterday, willing herself to jump.

She was just contemplating the weirdness of this when she rounded the corner and saw Mr. Webber hastily jumping back over the property line, a kid's bike dangling from one hand.

"Hey! What do you think you're doing?"

"Absolutely nothing," he said, face turning red just to underline the fact that he was lying.

"You and those damn kids need to stay out of my yard," Viv spat, feeling the anger roiling in her stomach.

"What makes you think that my grandchildren have been anywhere near your precious grass?"

"Um, the fact that you're standing there with a bike in your hand, one that was obviously just lying in my yard."

Webber rolled his eyes at her which just made her even madder. "You know your problem?" he said. "You're jealous."

"Me? Jealous? Of you?" As if. She rolled her eyes right on back.

"Damn right you are," Webber continued. "Jealous because I've got kids, because I've got a family and all you've got is a lonely old lady life." He was backing off into his own yard, dragging the bike with him.

"Jealous of you and your horrible kids? Right," Viv said. But her voice wasn't as strong as it had been before.

"You're a sad, lonely, weird lady. And you're grumpy and rude and it's no wonder no one can stand to be around you for long enough to have kids with you." He was almost in the open garage now.

Viv's mouth flapped open then closed. She could feel tightness in her chest. But she wasn't going to give him the satisfaction.

"Stay. Out. Of. My. Yard." The words came out staccato and

loud and then she turned on her heel and dragged Max away before the tears could come.

She made it all the way inside to the hallway before she lost control. All the way into her sad, lonely house that she shared with nobody before the crying started. And once it had started it was very, very hard to stop.

Max licked at her face.

"I know, I know," she sobbed. "I shouldn't let it get to me."

But it did get to her. It did because Mr. Webber was right. Things weren't supposed to be like this. She was thirty five. She and Bill should have had at least two kids by now. She should be living a bourgeois suburban life with her SUV and her school runs and her vacations at Disney that they both kept secret from the kids otherwise they wouldn't sleep at night.

Instead she was exactly what Webber had said. A lonely old woman.

She buried her face in her hands and let herself cry until her throat was raw and the tears dried up.

VIV CAME OUT of the bedroom, face still stinging from cold water, to find that Alice was standing in the hallway.

"What the fuck?"

"The door was unlocked," Alice said, blushing furiously. "I did knock, but no one answered and then, um, I thought maybe, well, okay, I shouldn't have come in."

"No," Viv said. "You shouldn't."

Alice peered closer. "Are you alright?"

"Fine, other than the fact that you're invading my house."

"Are you sure?" Alice asked. "Your eyes are red."

"Allergies. What's the plan for today?"

Alice narrowed her eyes then shrugged it off and Viv gave an internal sigh of relief. She definitely did not want to talk about feelings with Alice. Actually, she didn't want to talk about feelings at all. She was sick and tired of them and feelings were useless. She'd learned that a long time ago.

"Start small and practical," Alice said, beaming. "So we're going out for a walk. That's all. We'll see what happens along the way. We'll take pleasure in the small things. Want to bring Max along?"

Viv looked over to where Max was sleeping in the living room. He opened one lazy eye, closed it again, and shuffled into a more comfortable position.

"No, he's already had a walk this morning, he's tired."

"Fair enough, come on then, let's get out there and I want you to practice something for me. Smile, Viv, okay?"

Viv stretched her mouth into a grin.

"Jesus, maybe not quite so violently?" Alice said. "Just try to look pleasant, as though you're enjoying your walk. Sometimes the act of smiling can be enough to change the way we're feeling on the inside."

Viv stretched the grin even wider just out of spite as she followed Alice out of the house.

"I'm sorry about yesterday," Alice said as they began walking. "It wasn't well-planned of me and it definitely wasn't professional."

"I get that you wanted me to face my fears," Viv said, letting the manic grin drop. "Even I can kind of see the sense in that. But what on earth led you to start so big? I do have other fears, you know."

"Yes," said Alice. "Bananas. You mentioned them. Said they reminded you of penises. I thought you were being facetious."

"I was, kind of," Viv admitted. "But they are kind of phallic."

"I wouldn't know," Alice said, absently, she was studying their surroundings.

"Wouldn't know?" Viv asked, aware that she was prying. She knew that the girl was young, but even she couldn't be that much of a virgin, could she?

Alice flushed again. "Um, I'm more of an apple eater than a banana eater?"

"What... Oh, right, yes, Christ, sorry, didn't mean to offend or anything."

"No offense taken, you didn't know."

"Nor did I need to know. I'm sorry. I shouldn't have pried."

Alice shrugged. "I don't mind if you know things about me, Viv. That's how building a relationship works. You both have to give up a little bit of privacy in order to build trust."

Viv raised an eyebrow. "Is that what we're doing here, building a relationship?" After her confrontation with Mr. Webber this morning, this was a sore subject.

"Aren't we?" Alice asked. "I mean, I'm your life coach, so we already have a client and professional relationship. But does that mean we couldn't also build a friendly relationship, for example?"

"I guess not," Viv said doubtfully.

"Your life is very isolated, Viv. One of the things we need to work on is connecting with people."

"Eugh, seriously?"

"Yes," Alice said. "You need a social support system, we all do. That system is built up of tons of people, from the boy who brings your newspaper in the morning to your best friend in the world. Those interactions are important, they force you to see the world through someone else's eyes, they make you think of others, and they help you understand that others have the same problems as you, and that you can share problems with others."

"Christ," Viv said, this was starting to sound like therapy.

"I'm not asking a lot, Viv. I'm just asking that you're nice to some people."

"Nice?"

Alice wrinkled up her nose and Viv wanted to be annoyed at it but actually she looked kind of adorable. "You do come across as... thorny."

"Thorny?"

"Um, grumpy?" Alice provided.

"I can do nice," said Viv. "If I want to. The problem is, I just don't want to."

"I don't believe you."

"Obviously I can, I'm not completely socially hopeless."

"Fine," Alice said. "Then show me. Show me that you know how to be nice."

Viv looked around at the empty sidewalk. "How am I supposed to do that?"

Alice pointed behind Viv. "In there," she said.

Viv turned around to see a small, white building with large windows and a wooden sign out front. The local library. She sighed.

CHAPTER THIRTEEN

The foyer of the library was high-ceilinged and lit by sun coming through the big windows. It was quiet and calm, the air smelling like books and dust.

"What exactly am I supposed to do?" Viv hissed.

"Interact," Alice said airily. "Be nice, be pleasant, make a good first impression, and then come and tell me how you feel. It's that simple. There are plenty of people here. I'm not asking you to make best friends, simply say hello, talk about the weather, anything you like."

Viv frowned at her and for a moment Alice really did think that she was going to say no. But they had an agreement. This was definitely a baby step. And one that Alice truly thought Viv needed.

It was obvious that Viv had cut herself off from people. Whatever the reasons for that, Alice was sure that Viv would feel better about herself, about the world in general, once she started to re-establish contact.

"Fine," Viv huffed. And off she walked.

Alice leaned against a bookshelf and watched her go.

Something had upset her, Alice could see that. The red-tipped nose, the swollen eyes, Viv had clearly been crying, which was confusing, since Alice had been so sure that yesterday had ended well.

This was a process though, she reminded herself. One good

day didn't make for a whole good week.

Viv had sidled up to a woman in front of a rack of romance novels and whilst Alice could see that Viv's smile was false, the woman was genuinely smiling back, picking up a book and offering it to Viv.

Alice let herself relax a little. Okay, so this wasn't supposed to be her job, but it was going okay, she was stumbling her way through it. If she'd thought for one second that she was hurting Viv in any way, she'd have stopped, but as far as she could see, Viv was doing okay. Not great, but okay.

Over at the check-out desk, an older woman was scanning books, glasses sliding down her nose. Now, being married to a librarian couldn't be bad, Alice thought.

Quiet chats over books, a partner that knew everything or at least where to find everything, a calm person, Alice figured. A comfortable, quiet partnership.

She smiled for a second, but her eyes were drawn back inevitably to Viv, who was now discussing something with a man standing in front of a community noticeboard. She looked to be talking a lot, but the guy didn't look as though he was being harangued.

Married to someone like Viv, though, that would be an experience. Quiet wouldn't be the word Alice would choose for that. Exciting, maybe, volatile perhaps, Viv would call her out on her mistakes, but in the end would support her through everything. Whatever other faults Viv might have, Alice suspected that she was loyal to a fault once a connection was made.

She was attractive too, especially now that she was smiling. Alice could see a dimple in her cheek, the way her eyes crinkled at the corners. Not to mention comforting. She couldn't imagine having made that damn jump yesterday with anyone else.

"Your wife?"

Alice jumped. "What? Sorry?"

The librarian with the glasses was standing beside her, not quite as old as Alice had thought now that she was up close. "Is that your wife?" she asked again.

"What? Who? That?" Alice said, aware that she was sounding not-quite-right. But the idea of her and Viv... Just the idea...

An idea that she'd literally just been contemplating.

A thought that for the very first time had crossed her mind.

Unlike every other woman in the world, Alice hadn't considered Viv in that way. Until just this moment.

She shook her head. "No, no," she assured the librarian.

"Oh, I'm sorry," the woman said, looking abashed. "I just assumed... I mean, the way you were watching her, I, uh, I never should have said anything."

Alice smiled at her. "Don't worry," she said. "I'm the same. Spotting another gay couple in public can be the high point of my day. It kind of makes me want to wave my arms around and say 'me too,' you know?"

The librarian grinned. "Yeah, I know. I definitely jumped the gun on that one though, I am sorry."

"Don't be," Alice said. "As a matter of fact, Viv over there is my client. I'm a life coach. She's practicing, um, being nice to people, I suppose."

"Uh-huh," said the librarian. She turned so that she could watch Viv too. "It's better than practicing being horrible to people, I guess."

"Yeah, I'm not sure Viv needs practice in that. I'm Alice," Alice said, holding out her hand.

"Caroline, most people call me Cal."

"Pleasure to meet you."

"You know, I'm not sure we've had life coaching in the library before," Cal said. "Crocheting, knitting, book club, city planning, even cooking, but not life coaching."

"Ah," Alice said. "It wasn't exactly planned. We just happened to be outside when the time came, so we came in. I hope it's okay, I didn't mean to bother people."

"Not at all, it's completely fine. I'm happy to have people come through the doors, whatever the reason," said Cal, smiling. Then the smile dropped away from her face. "Although, I'm not entirely sure how well your coaching is going currently."

Alice turned to see Viv striding toward her, face grim and clouded, cheeks flushed with anger. "Oh, dear," she said, just before Viv came into hearing distance.

"It's ridiculous, absolutely ridiculous," Viv said.

"What is?" asked Alice. "And please don't shout, Viv, this is a library."

"This deserves to be shouted," said Viv, putting her hands on her hips.

Her eyes were flashing and her hair was mussed up and Alice had another sudden thought, one that she'd definitely never entertained before. A thought that involved flushed cheeks and flashing eyes and messed up hair and breathlessness and... She cleared her throat.

No.

Not this time.

Not again.

Viv was a client. Viv was straight. Viv was absolutely off limits. And Alice was just being her usual silly self and imagining relationships that didn't exist.

"What deserves to be shouted?" she asked quietly and, she hoped, calmly.

"Do you know that they're planning on closing this place down?" she asked. She turned to Cal. "Did you know?" she said, almost accusingly.

"I'm the head librarian," said Cal. "So, yes, actually, I did know."

"And nobody's doing a thing about it!" Viv shrieked.

"Who said nobody's doing anything about it?" Cal asked. "As a matter of fact, we're holding a fundraiser next week, and we're doing everything we can to come up with new ideas to keep the library open."

Viv's face calmed a little. "You are? But why aren't there posters on the noticeboard about it then? Or, I don't know, brainstorming meetings?"

Cal sighed. "Yes, we could be a little more organized, I suppose. It's just that all this came out of the blue and we're on such a short time schedule." She paused and looked at Viv over her glasses. "I don't suppose you'd like to help, would you?"

"Yes," Viv said defiantly. She stared at Alice as though daring her to say something.

Alice shrugged. "Sure. We can both help."

"Great, there's a meeting the day after tomorrow, we can call that a brainstorming meeting, and we'll be talking about the fundraiser too, just come on by here around seven."

She grinned at them both then hurried off to help someone at the desk.

"Since when have you been so interested in libraries?" Alice asked. It had been odd to see Viv passionate about something. Nice, but different, not at all what she'd expected.

"You're the one that wanted me to make connections with people," said Viv.

"Yes," Alice said. "But this seems... kind of out of character, if you don't mind me saying so."

"You know what really grinds my gears?" Viv said. "Cheating. Unfairness, but mostly cheating. Cheating of any kind. Cheating like my asshole of an ex-husband, cheating on your taxes, cheating to win, any kind of cheating."

"Okay," said Alice slowly, unsure of where this was going.

"And this is cheating," said Viv. "Pure and simple. It's the town council cheating people out of a fine resource, one that belongs to everyone, simply so they can spend more money on, what? Roads? Guns? Who the hell knows."

"Right," Alice said. "I kind of get that, I suppose. But are you sure you're up to this? Meetings, other people, breaking out of your shell?"

"Isn't this what you and Evie wanted?" Viv said. "Me getting back out there, me leaving my couch?"

"Well, yes," Alice said.

"Then shut up and let's finish this walk so we can go home and come up with ideas for how to keep this place open," said Viv, stalking out of the library.

Alice took a breath. Unexpected. Or maybe not. Viv was

obviously still hurt and angry about her divorce. Maybe this was a way for her to punish cheaters everywhere. Maybe she did need this. At the very least it would get her out of the house.

She wasn't sure if this was part of life coaching or not. But then again, what did she know? And a project did seem like it might be helpful for Viv.

And maybe for Alice too.

Anything to keep her mind off the suddenly weird thoughts she'd been having about her client.

CHAPTER FOURTEEN

She hadn't lied. The closing of the library really did strike her as unfair. And it was cheating. Rich bureaucrats looking to cheat regular people out of a local institution so that they could spend more on the things that were less important. At least to Viv's mind.

Not that there wasn't an ulterior motive here.

The library project was just the thing, she'd realized as soon as she'd heard of the closing. It gave her something to work on, a reason to get out of the house, and, most importantly, it would keep Alice from planning any more bungee jumps or whatever the hell else she had in mind.

This could, Viv thought, tick more than one box. She wanted to help, she thought libraries were important. She also didn't want to be forced into sky-diving. Or Scuba diving. Or any other kind of diving.

As for the terms of her deal with both Alice and Evie, well, she was making an effort. If at the end of that effort, library closed or open, she ended up back on her couch watching the Discovery Channel, well, so be it. She could try for a little while longer.

"What about a read-a-thon?" Alice said.

They were sitting on the living room floor, paper spread out on the coffee table in front of them. "What's a read-a-thon?" Viv asked.

"Uh, I don't really know," said Alice. "But it sounds like a thing.

And lots of fundraising stuff has 'a-thon' added to the end."

"And this is a library," Viv finished for her. Alice was smiling and Viv shook her head. "You're smiling again. Stop it. If you smile so much then people won't know when you really mean it."

"So you save smiles up in case they're needed?" Alice asked.

"No, I don't use them unnecessarily. I don't want people thinking I'm nice or kind or a pushover or anything else. I bet you get taken advantage of all the time."

"I don't think so," said Alice. "I guess sometimes people will take too much, but that's the nature of people, not the nature of me. Besides, I'd rather be scammed a little every now and again than be closed off and refuse to help if people need it."

"Hey, I'm helping here," Viv said.

"I didn't say you weren't, I just pointed out that being smiley too much isn't as bad as being grumpy too much."

"Grumpy keeps away the gold-diggers, beggars, and scam artists."

"Gold-diggers been a big problem in your life, have they?" asked Alice innocently.

Viv growled. "You know what I mean."

"I know that you deliberately paint a gruff façade so that you can protect yourself."

"A big brick wall to cover up the gooey center?" Viv said, rolling her eyes.

"Mock it if you will, but I've got your number, Vivien Curtis. You're nowhere near as horrible as you'd like people to believe you are."

"On that note, I've got yours," said Viv. "I don't think you're anywhere near as nice as you'd like people to believe."

"I am," Alice said, looking up and smiling again. "I just am."

"No bodies buried in the back yard?" Viv asked. "Never lied?"

"Not a big one, no, only social ones."

"Never cheated?"

Alice shook her head.

"Never faked an orgasm?"

Alice blushed bright red and Viv laughed, not unkindly.

"I'm kidding with you. But no one is perfect. We all have our moments. You're not Mother Teresa, I'm pretty sure of that."

"I never said I was," Alice grumbled, picking up her phone and tapping something into it. "Hey, look at this, a read-a-thon is a thing. People get sponsored to read as many pages as they can and then the sponsors pay out."

"No shit," Viv said, shuffling around the table until she was next to Alice and could see her phone screen. "Huh. Who'd have thought? Put that on the list of ideas then."

Alice bent to add to the list and her arm brushed against Viv's.

For a second, a sparkly feeling filled her up, warm and fizzy and she thought she might be getting sick. Then Alice moved again and her arm brushed against Viv's again and the same fizzy feeling came back.

"You spelled it wrong," Viv said, intentionally leaning in closer.

Her arm pressed against Alice's.

"No, I didn't."

The pressure was growing inside her, the warmth, the... naturalness of being touched, of touching. She backed off, unsure of what was happening, nearly frightened by what was happening. "No," she said. "You didn't. My bad."

But she was looking at Alice's profile now, the sharpness of her nose, the smattering of freckles, the way her blonde hair was tucked behind the delicate curl of her ear.

Jesus fucking Christ.

No way.

But the warmth traveled all the way down through her stomach and further until there was no doubt at all in Viv's mind that she was beginning to get turned on.

Her breath caught in her throat for a second.

"What?" Alice said, turning to look at her.

"Nothing," Viv said, scrambling to her feet. "More coffee?"

"Sure."

And she escaped to the kitchen, where Max was snoring in

contentment in a patch of sunshine.

"What the fuck?" she whispered.

She flicked the coffee machine on, letting the water bubble again.

"It's nothing," she told herself sternly.

And it wasn't. Everyone had stray thoughts every now and again. And she hadn't been laid for, well, for years at this point. Hadn't been touched for nearly as long. It was only natural. Maybe this was part of the process. Maybe this was part of her coming back to life again, regaining herself. This awakening of libido, this return of feelings.

Feelings, in general, were stupid. But she'd almost forgotten about these kinds of feelings. The warm, squirmy kind of feelings.

Perhaps she'd just been numb for so long that any touch, no matter who it came from, was enough to push her over an edge.

She peered through into the living room, where Alice was bent over their list of ideas.

She certainly hoped so.

Because being involved with Little Miss Sunshine professionally was bad enough. Imagine having to wake up next to a smile like that every damn morning.

"HOW'S LONDON?" VIV laid back on her bed, muting the TV with the remote.

"As rainy as expected," Evie said. "But pretty awesome, to be honest."

"Good, I'm glad," said Viv, yawning. "You know that it's like eleven at night here, right?"

"Yeah, I'm sorry, jet-lag and all that. I just wanted to hear your voice, that's all."

"Getting all lonely over there in Merry Old England?" teased Viv.

"Maybe, a little."

"You should have taken Greg then, rather than just going it

alone. Didn't he want to go too?"

Greg was Evie's husband. A nice enough guy, in Viv's opinion, though the two of them weren't particularly close. He and Evie clearly adored each other, and that was enough for Viv. But now she was thinking about it, it was kind of odd that the two hadn't gone together.

"There was no point for such a short time," Evie said.

There was something in her voice that Viv didn't like. But before she could say anything, Evie asked how she was doing.

"Aha, calling to check up on me," Viv said. "I should have thought as much. Your secret is uncovered."

"No, well, yes, maybe, a little," Evie laughed. "Are you alright?"

"Fine."

"And the life coaching?" pressed Evie.

"Fine."

"Don't I get a little more than that?"

Viv sighed. She'd worked hard to banish the thought of Alice from her mind all evening. After the weirdness of the afternoon she'd never quite got back on track. She'd gone back to being grumpy, since that was safest, and eventually Alice had left her alone.

Whatever hormonal thing it was that had gone on, Viv was determined to forget about it. And discussing Alice with Evie didn't seem like the way to go about that.

"It's all fine," she said. "I did a bungee jump. Well, a fake one. Oh, and I'm going to help run a fundraiser.

"Huh," Evie said. "It sounds like you're a whole new woman already, and I've only been gone a few days. This life coach guy must be pretty amazing."

Viv bit her lip and didn't correct her. It was a passing moment, a decision made so quickly she barely thought about it. Right then, it didn't seem important at all.

"Tell me the three most British things that you've seen so far," she said, snuggling down onto the bed. "And also, have you been practicing your fake accent yet? Because if you don't come back with one, I'm going to be pissed."

Evie laughed and started to tell Viv about her experiences. And Viv sank into the comfort of her voice, barely thinking about Alice even once for the next hour. Or at least not twice. Definitely not three times.

CHAPTER FIFTEEN

Alice shrugged out of her jacket and collapsed at the kitchen table.

"So?" Harrison asked. "How was your day?"

"Well, we're saving a library, which is unexpected. But then again, we didn't jump off anything higher than a porch step, so I'd call that a win."

"You're saving a library?"

"Um, yes. Or attempting to." Alice rubbed at her face. "How about your day?"

Harrison sighed. "No job yet. But the interview this afternoon went pretty well, I think. I've got another tomorrow, so we'll see. I'm keeping my fingers crossed that we'll be out of this hole pretty soon."

"You got this," Alice grinned. "You're going to be just fine."

"And I can see how you can be a great life coach," smiled Harrison back. "You and all your extra positivity."

"Do you think I smile too much?"

"What?"

"Just something Viv keeps saying," said Alice, frowning. "She says I smile too much."

"Ignore her. You smile just the perfect amount. Besides, who's the teacher here and who's the pupil? You should be telling her to smile more."

"I did. She gave me a grin that could have scared a grown man from fifty feet," said Alice.

Harrison was clicking around on her laptop. "You know, this life coaching thing is actually a real thing," she said. "You can get certifications and everything. It's not all as up-in-the-air as I thought."

"Oh, I know," said Alice. "Trust me. I checked out everything I could find online. I needed to get some clue as to what I'm doing here. But Foster doesn't have any of these qualifications at all, I did check."

"Which doesn't mean you couldn't get one," said Harrison. "Or even a psych degree, if you wanted to take this really seriously."

Alice laughed. "Are you really planning a whole new career for me? This is just temporary, remember? I'm technically only an assistant."

"Yes, but you seem to be enjoying yourself, bungee jumping aside. And, well, I can see how you could be really good at this, Al. You're positive, you're encouraging. Don't tell me that you wouldn't like a job where you just help people live their best lives all the time."

"Yes, I guess. Maybe. I don't know." She rubbed her face again, she was tired. "I do know that it's kind of exhausting. I also know that I need a bath and an early night."

"Go on then," said Harrison. "Bathroom's all yours. Shall I bring you a glass of wine? Just to help you sleep."

"You, my dear, would make the perfect wife," said Alice getting up.

"I wish you'd tell that to every single man in a fifty block radius," grumbled Harrison, closing her laptop. "Still not in love with your client yet?"

Alice's skin prickled and her mouth went dry. "Absolutely not."

"That's got to be a first for you," Harrison grinned, grabbing a wine bottle from the fridge. "Go and run that bath, I'll bring you a glass."

ALICE RUSHED INTO the library, knowing that she was running late and cursing herself for not being there when Viv needed her.

She'd known all about the meeting, obviously. She'd helped Viv prepare, helped her come up with fundraising ideas. Then she'd escaped to go visit Foster, mostly because she still felt sorry for him having no one else.

Unfortunately, gall-bladder removed, he was now even more cranky than before. He'd called her Anthea, Annie, and Aleisha repeatedly, and had talked her ear off about what she should be doing with 'his' client. She'd only managed to tear herself away from the hospital by telling him she had an evening coaching session starting.

The library was well-lit and she could hear voices coming from a side room, so she made a bee-line for it, stopping in the doorway when she recognized that it was Viv's voice she could hear more than anything.

Viv was standing in front of a white-board, explaining how the read-a-thon would work. She was smiling, her hair sticking up from where she'd run her hands through it, but holding the attention of everyone in the small room.

Alice leaned against the door-frame, watching her, seeing the sparkle in her eyes. She had no idea, she realized now, what Viv had done before she got married, or even during her marriage. She assumed that there had been a career, a job at least.

Maybe that was what Viv needed to get her life back. Some kind of meaning, some reason to get up in the morning.

Viv was answering a question and Alice must have caught her eye, because she gave a half-wave and a distracted smile and Alice's heart jumped in response.

And just like that she was spun back into the sweaty, breathlessness of her dream. She'd woken at three, panting, body tight, with a very, very clear image of what she'd been dreaming. An image of Viv, pushing her up against a wall, Viv running her hands over Alice's hips, Viv leaning in closer to wrap her fingers in Alice's hair to drag her in...

It was dark and quiet in the apartment and Alice's breath had been coming raw and ragged and her hands had moved of their own accord. She just hadn't been able to help herself.

Then afterward she had felt uncomfortable with herself and had found it impossible to sleep again.

All hormonal, she told herself. Just that time of the month, that was all. That coupled with the fact that she pictured every woman as a partner. Not generally in quite so much detail though...

Viv had finished talking and sat down, so Alice snuck in and grabbed a seat by the door, just as Cal was getting up to discuss the details of the coming fundraiser.

"We've got invitations already printed," she said. "So if you could take a stack on your way out and pass them around, that'd be great. I just wanted to remind you that whilst it will be held here at the library it is black tie, so dress appropriately. Most of the town council will be here, thanks to free food and drink."

There was some chuckling at this.

"And we've finally got our website up and running, thanks to Tom over here, who just wants a quick word with everyone."

A man stood up that Alice recognized as the person Viv had been talking to two days ago by the library noticeboard. Cal came to sit one seat down from Alice, a dark-haired woman in between them.

"Well done, darling," whispered the dark-haired woman to Cal.

Cal turned around and saw Alice. "Well hey there, I didn't know if you'd be coming."

"I was running late, sorry," Alice whispered.

Cal grinned. "This is my wife, Lea," she whispered back. The dark-haired woman turned and smiled. "Lea, this is Alice, she's here with Viv."

"Oh, what a cute couple," Lea squeaked.

"No, no," said Alice hurriedly. "We're not together."

Lea blushed and Cal giggled a little and then they all hushed up to hear about the website.

Not the first time she and Viv had been mistaken for a couple, Alice thought. They would make a cute couple, Lea wasn't wrong about that. Her long blonde hair against Viv's short dark hair. Her pale skin against Viv's olive skin. Her...

Her breath was coming faster again.

For God's sake.

First priority upon getting a day off was to get a date. Any date. With any one. Anything to get this out of her system.

The meeting finally wound up and Alice stretched the kinks out of her back before finding Viv.

"Sorry I was late," she said. "I got caught up at the hospital."

"The hospital?" Viv said with a look of alarm.

"It's fine, just a... a friend," said Alice. "But you looked great out there. Confident. You even smiled."

"I can smile when I want to," scowled Viv.

"Right, I know that. And it's just as well, since you appear to have picked up a hundred invitations to this fundraiser."

"So?"

"So, you're going to have to hand those out and ask people to come," Alice said. "Which is going to be a lot more successful if you actually smile."

"For fuck's sake," Viv said in dismay, looking down at the handful of invites she'd grabbed.

"It's a good experience," Alice said comfortingly. "And it's about time you met some of your neighbors. There's a strong correlation between neighbors who recognize each other and neighborhood security, as well as neighborhood satisfaction surveys."

"No way," Viv said immediately.

Alice took a breath and then decided that she didn't have the energy. Not tonight. Not after waking up at three in the morning.

So she bit her tongue instead and let Viv usher her out of the building toward her car.

It was dark already, the shadows creeping along the parking lot, and quiet too, like they were the only people in the world.

Viv walked her all the way to the car, then nodded, but didn't move.

"Good night," said Alice, wishing that Viv would move and praying that she'd stay right where she was.

Viv looked at her for a long moment, longer than was comfortable, long enough that warmth built up in Alice's stomach, long enough that she subconsciously began to lean forward.

Then Viv was stepping back. "Night," she said, and walked off.

CHAPTER SIXTEEN

"**I** thought this is what you wanted?" Viv said, holding the phone to her ear with her shoulder and struggling to pull on a pair of jeans.

"It is what I wanted," Evie said. "I'm just not so sure it's what I want."

"Okay, Little Miss Decisive," said Viv, finally pulling the jeans on. "If you don't like it, come home."

"It's not that simple." There was a pause on the end of the line that Viv didn't like.

"Then tell me why not. Tell me what's going on."

"It's... It's nothing, Viv. Really. What about your coaching, how's that going?"

Viv rolled her eyes. Evie told her everything. Eventually. Sometimes it took a while though. There was obviously something going on, and Viv had a whole store of things to say about being careful what you wish for. But Evie wasn't ready yet to admit that she didn't like London.

Fine, she could play along for now.

"It's going fine. We're saving a library."

"You're... saving a library. That's what I'm paying for?"

"Actually, yes. If I send you a link, could you make a donation? It's for a really good cause, Eve, promise." There was a knock at the door. "And I gotta run. There's someone at the door."

"Aren't you a little social butterfly," Evie said approvingly. "Go on then. Off you go. Don't forget to send me the link."

Viv threw the phone on the bed and went to get the door. Alice was standing, the sunlight catching on her hair, and Viv suddenly wanted to hug her. Which she didn't, obviously.

"So, you're here then."

"Here and ready to go invite people to this fundraiser. Make sure you're wearing good shoes," Alice said. "There's going to be a lot of walking and you don't want blisters."

Viv groaned, but pulled on her old sneakers. Max, sensing a walk, snuffled into the hallway. "Come on then, Maxie, if I have to do this, you might as well come too. You'll make a decent ice-breaker as long as you remember not to pee on people's trash cans."

And pretty soon they were all three walking along the sidewalk to the beginning of the route that Alice had planned.

"I've been meaning to ask you," Alice said. "Did you work? Before you got married, I mean."

"Huh," laughed Viv. "I worked while I was married. The only reason I don't now is because I had a good lawyer and I scalped that asshole for all I could get and then..." she sighed. "And then I didn't really know what to do."

"What did you do? Before, I mean."

"You'll laugh."

"I won't."

"I worked in PR." She side-eyed Alice just in case she was going to laugh. But she didn't.

"Your people skills should be on-point then," was all Alice said. "If a little rusty."

"Maybe." Max trotted along beside her. "What about you?" she asked, finally. "I know nothing about you at all. Or is that breaking some kind of life coach rule or something?"

Alice looked hesitant, then shook her head. "There's not much to know. I'm twenty five, single, grew up in the mid-west and now I'm working as a life coach. Not exactly a thrilling tale."

"That's all I'm getting?"

"There's no more to tell," Alice laughed. "I'm really not an exciting person at all."

"You could have fooled me," Viv said, the words slipping out of her mouth before she could stop them. Mostly because she was curious about Alice, curious how someone a decade younger than her could be handing out advice. Handing out, as it turned out, fairly decent advice. "How did you end up as a life coach?"

"Hmm?"

"How come you're a life coach? Where did you train? What got you into it?" Viv said.

"It's a long story," was all Alice said. Then she stopped abruptly in front of a house on the corner of the street. "And this is where the work starts. Off you go then. Dust off those people skills and get to inviting. Don't forget to smile and be friendly."

Viv groaned, but took a pile of invitations from Alice's tote bag. "Fine," she said.

"The fate of the library is in your hands," Alice reminded her.

Viv groaned again, but painted a smile on her face as she walked up the first driveway.

VIV'S FEET ACHED AND her face hurt from smiling, but they were almost home now, and she managed to speed up a little.

"Not so fast," said Alice, holding out an invite.

"What's that?" Viv asked, stopping in the middle of the sidewalk. Max immediately lay down.

"There's one more invitation. It's for your neighbor."

Viv looked at Webber's house and then back at Alice. "Nope. No way, no how. Not going to happen. Nein. Non. I've run out of languages, but you get the idea."

"Yes," Alice said, firmly. "It's about time you mend fences. The two of you live next door to each other, this little war you're carrying on is ridiculous. You could really help each other out, especially if you're going on vacation or something and need plants watering or the house watching."

"As if," Viv said.

"Yes, as if. It's polite. And the more people that come to the fundraiser, the better. You're all of, what, thirty something, and you're already acting like the weird old lady that won't give the kids their ball back when it comes in her yard."

"What's wrong with that? It's my yard."

"It's bad for your blood pressure. And you're taking out your lousy attitude on kids so young they can barely walk. Shame on you."

"It's my yard," Viv said again, more loudly this time.

There was a moment of stillness, then Alice laid a hand on Viv's arm and that funny fizzing feeling started again and all of a sudden, Viv knew exactly what it was, exactly where she'd felt it before. Back in eleventh grade in the front seat of Bill's father's Chevy truck when Bill turned his cap around and leaned in, the smell of gum minty on his breath, and kissed her for the very first time.

She snatched her arm away in shock and, not knowing what else to do, she grabbed the invitation from Alice's hand. "Fine," she said. Anything to walk away from the fizzing feeling.

Her hand was trembling when she knocked on the door, but facing Webber wasn't what scared her.

"What?" Webber said, cracking the door open.

"Here," said Viv, thrusting the invitation at him.

"Is it loaded with anthrax or something?" Webber asked, suspiciously.

"No, it's an invite to a fundraiser for the library down the block," she said, feeling Alice's eyes on her from behind.

"A fundraiser?" asked Webber, opening the door fully. "Why?"

"They're thinking of closing the place."

"No shit. I go there all the time. My grandkids love going there. They can't close it down."

"Then come to the fundraiser, help out. There's an auction and stuff."

"And you're helping to organize this?"

Viv shrugged, then nodded.

"Not quite the wicked witch of the west then, are you?" He narrowed his eyes at her. "You know, I tell the kids not to go on your lawn. But they're little, they don't always get it. And there's no fence or anything."

Viv nodded. "Yeah, I suppose that's understandable. I just... You know, I've got a dog. I worry about the kids and the dog. And sometimes there's dog poop on the lawn. I mean, I clean it up, but I might not get to it immediately. And I wouldn't want the kids..." she trailed off.

Webber nodded. "Yeah, understandable. I could maybe keep a closer eye on them."

"I could keep a closer eye on Max, my dog, too," she said. She wiped her arm across her forehead. "It's not such a huge deal if they come over. Just as long as they're careful. I mean, if they wanted to get their ball or something." She thought of Alice's words.

"Yeah, okay, great," said Webber. He looked down at the invitation. "So, I suppose I'll see you at this thing then?"

Viv nodded and finally managed a smile as Webber closed the door.

"Did you just... make peace with your neighbor?" Alice said, eyes wide with surprise as Viv reached the end of the drive.

"Uh, yeah, maybe, I think."

"Woo-hoo," cried Alice and Viv's smile broadened into a grin. "I knew you could do it. Nice work!"

And before Viv knew what was happening, Alice was pulling her into a hug and suddenly all the feelings came. The warmth and scent of Alice filled her up and she was so confused and wrong-footed, but at the same time she couldn't pull herself away.

"I'm proud of you," Alice said, pulling back and letting her go. "Now why don't we get poor Max inside and get you a well-deserved drink."

"Uh-huh," Viv squeaked. She coughed, cleared her throat. "Better make it a big one."

CHAPTER SEVENTEEN

S he regretted the hug. If only because it affirmed what she'd begun to think. Something that she didn't really want to think about at all, if only because Foster Davison would kill her if he found out.

"My feet are killing me," Viv said, kicking off her shoes and sinking onto the couch.

"You did good work though," said Alice. "Want me to get something from the kitchen? Water maybe?"

"To hell with that," said Viv. "There's a bottle of wine on the rack by the refrigerator. Bring that, two glasses, and the corkscrew from the drawer by the sink."

"Yes, mistress," Alice said, then wished she hadn't because a strange look fluttered across Viv's face. "I, uh, mean, sure, of course."

In the kitchen, she fanned herself with a stray place-mat while she found the wine and glasses. What was she playing at here? This was work. This was a client. This was what she was depending on to pay the rent.

Throw in the fact that Viv was presumably straight, in a vulnerable position, and didn't even know half the truth about who Alice really was, and any kind of feelings were way out of order.

Alice steeled herself and went back into the living room. Time to be professional.

"So," she said, sitting on the armchair and depositing the glasses and bottle on the table. "How are you feeling? We've done a lot, you've had a lot of people-contact, you're involved in something to help the community. It looks like you're breaking out of your shell. But how does all that leave you feeling?"

Viv stuck her tongue out. "Really? We're going down the 'how does that make you feel' route?"

"I'd like to know," Alice said. If only to know whether she was actually helping or not.

"Fine," said Viv, sticking the corkscrew into the wine bottle and twisting it. "I feel... good, I guess."

"Good, you guess?"

She pulled the cork out of the bottle with a pop. "You know, I have done therapy. I know how this works. The whole repeating things back to me, I've had that before."

"Did it work?"

"What do you think?" scowled Viv. "I'm sitting here with you, aren't I?" Then her face cleared. "Though, to be honest, you've accomplished a hell of a lot more than anyone else I've talked to."

"I'm not sure that's me," Alice said. "Maybe it was just time, maybe you just needed a helping hand to get out of the situation you found yourself in."

"Maybe," Viv said, pouring wine. "And, in answer to your question, I feel... better, I think. Lighter maybe. It's easier to sleep. Getting out and doing something is easier than I thought it'd be. I knew that I needed to do something, I just didn't know what."

"That's good," Alice said, as she accepted a glass. "It's good to know that you're feeling better."

"I just, I kind of went into a funk," said Viv. "And you're right, it was hard to get out of. I'm not saying I'm out of it now. But I feel like I might be on my way. Bill leaving was, well, it was the right thing but that didn't mean it didn't hurt."

"Not having life turn out the way you expected it to can be

difficult," said Alice. She looked down into the dark wine. She was only twenty five. Her dreams weren't lost. She knew that. But it was tough sometimes, not having anyone, not having the partner she craved for.

"No shit," said Viv. "But I'm doing okay now, I think. And that's thanks to you, Little Miss Sunshine." She raised her glass. "I know I'm a grump, and I know I don't make things easy, but thank you for helping me. I mean that."

Alice leaned forward and tapped her glass against Viv's and felt a sudden surge of guilt. She sighed.

"Actually, Viv, there's something you should know."

"You're an undercover FBI agent?" Viv asked.

"Um, no, though where you'd get that idea I don't know."

"You're the last person anyone would take for an FBI agent, which makes you the perfect undercover agent," Viv said, settling back on the couch with her wine.

"No, not even close," said Alice. She took a sip of wine. "Uh, well, I'm not exactly a life coach."

Viv frowned. "What?"

"I'm kind of an assistant life coach?" Alice said. She sighed again. "Okay, here's the deal. Your friend Evie hired Foster Davison, who is a life coach. He hired me to be his assistant. And then he went and had some kind of old lady gall-bladder attack and left me holding the reins."

"You're his assistant," Viv said.

Alice nodded and then held her breath because Viv had every right to be angry with her, every right to throw her out, to report her to Foster, to do whatever she wanted. She'd misrepresented herself, and only right now did she really understand what a horrible thing that had been to do.

Then Viv laughed.

Actually laughed.

Laughed in a way that filled Alice's heart up and made it beat harder, in a way that made her smile even though it was the last thing she wanted to do, in a way that made her gulp down half a glass of wine just to try and stop the reactions she was having.

"Jesus Christ," Viv said, wiping her eyes. "That's the funniest fucking thing I've ever heard. You must have been sweating bullets trying to figure out how to fake your way through this."

"Well, I did have info from the office," Alice said. "And from the internet."

Viv shrugged. "Well, it's the results that speak, not the method. I'm feeling better than I have in months and that's down to you, life coach or not. Maybe you should think about asking for a promotion."

Alice smiled weakly. Somehow, she didn't think Foster would see things the same way.

SHE SANK INTO the couch and Harrison flicked the TV off. "What is it?"

Alice looked at her roommate. "I've made a terrible, horrible, awful mistake."

Harrison's face paled. "Jesus, please tell me you haven't killed anyone."

Alice sat up straighter. "What is it with people today? Viv thought I was an undercover FBI agent, now you think I've killed someone."

"It's always the quiet ones," Harrison said. "And you can be pretty quiet."

"No, I'm not in the FBI, and I haven't killed anyone."

"What is it then?" asked Harrison, crossing her legs.

Alice swallowed hard, she couldn't not talk about this, but the idea of it made her stomach flutter. "I, um, well, it's Viv."

Harrison rolled her eyes. "You've fallen for her, haven't you?"

"No," said Alice. "Well, maybe. Yes. I don't know. But it's not like you think."

Harrison patted her leg. "Chill, Al. It's fine. You do this all the time, you know that it's nothing. So you imagined her painting the nursery, or dressed in a wedding dress, or working in the garden. It's no big deal."

"That's the thing," Alice said, heart throbbing. "I didn't

imagine her doing any of those things."

"Wait, you didn't just think about playing wife with her?" Harrison asked, voice worried now.

Alice shook her head. "It was more, um, intimate. And then sometimes she touches me, not on purpose, accidentally, or brushes by me, or like today we hugged because she did something great and..." She didn't finish the sentence.

"You like her," Harrison said. "As in really like her."

Alice nodded.

"Crap."

"Thanks, that's helpful."

Harrison grimaced. "Is she into you?"

"That's moot. She's a client, she's probably straight, and she's a decade older than me, and... So many other things."

"There's only one thing you can do," said Harrison. "You need to back off. If she's not interested, then it's inappropriate, and you need to walk away from this."

"I can't, this is my job, we've got rent to pay and all that. Besides, Foster won't be ready to work again for at least ten days."

Harrison blew out her cheeks in thought. "Then I guess you have to be careful, make sure you're not touching or doing anything you shouldn't be doing. And get away from the situation as soon as you can. You're an adult, you can control yourself around this woman, right?"

"Of course I can," Alice said. "I'm not going to do anything to her, who do you think I am?"

"Then be cautious," Harrison said. "I know that's not the ideal solution, and I know from experience how hard it can be to work around someone you're attracted to. But you've gotta steer clear of her as much as you can."

Which would be fine if they weren't working one on one, Alice thought. She nodded again. "Yeah, I'll be careful." She sniffed. "I really wasn't expecting this to happen."

Harrison rubbed her leg. "You're not at fault here. It's a rough deal, but you'll get through it and when you do, we'll find you a proper date, okay?"

Which reminded Alice that she really needed to find a dress for the fundraiser. "Have you got a black dress?"

"Nope," Harrison said. "But I do have a red one."

Alice groaned. Appearing at a fundraiser in a red dress. Just the ticket for not attracting attention to herself.

CHAPTER EIGHTEEN

V iv drew the line at being picked up for the fundraiser.

It was all very well that Alice wanted to be supportive, and she could understand why Alice might think she'd turn tail and run. But she wasn't getting picked up.

She wasn't a child, this wasn't a date, it's not like they were going to prom. And she certainly wasn't getting picked up by someone who gave her fizzy feelings that left her confused and slightly worried.

She pulled on pantyhose, biting her tongue to ensure that they didn't run and that she kept her patience.

This whole thing was a shit-show. Not the fundraiser. Not even getting dressed up like some kind of penguin. But whatever the hell was going on here.

On the one hand, she felt better than she had in months. Years, probably. Alice had been just the catalyst she needed to get out of herself, to finally start trying to live again. Although Evie had helped, to be fair. The thought of being without Evie, the thought of her going away, had been a wake up call. And the thought of Evie giving up something she'd longed for to stay for her had made her feel nauseous.

Not that it looked like there was much chance of Evie staying in London now. She was sounding more and more down with every phone call. It wasn't lost on Viv that the better she was starting to feel, the worse Evie was getting.

On the other hand, Alice was... confusing.

And Viv didn't like being confused.

No, she wanted straight-forward, easy to understand clarity.

She snorted to herself a little as she remembered Alice's confession. Not even a life coach. The idea tickled her somehow, the thought of organized Alice being thrown into the deep end.

Maybe she should be mad about that. But how could she be? Alice had clearly helped her, it wouldn't be fair to criticize her now just because she was missing some kind of certificate or whatever.

Although, tossing Alice out of her life would be one way of solving her current problem.

She finished buttoning up her shirt, did up her pants, then pulled on her jacket.

"What do you think, Max?" she asked.

Max was lying on the bed. He opened one eye then promptly closed it again.

"Thanks for your support," muttered Viv as she grabbed her purse and cell phone. If she didn't leave now she'd be late.

* * *

Alice pushed her feet into sharp high heels and Harrison tutted.

"Keep still, I'm just getting the last few strands right."

"Sorry," said Alice, standing as still as she could.

"There you go," Harrison said, finally. "Wow. You're a knock-out."

Alice looked in the mirror and gulped. The dress was red, very red. It was also tight and cut low enough that she could see the gentle rise of her breasts and the line of her breastbone. It clung to every curve. There could be no secrets in this dress.

What was she thinking?

She was making an idiot of herself in a dress like this. And yet... and yet she wanted Viv to see it. Wanted her to know what she was missing even though Viv was probably missing nothing at all.

Which was dumb.

She should change.

"Uh, no," Harrison said, as Alice started to turn toward her room. "You look fantastic. Besides, you're already running late. There's no time to change. Go on. You've got an Uber waiting downstairs."

Alice flashed a scowl at her, but she was right. She had to go.

Crap.

She just hoped that everyone else was as dressed up as she was.

She just hoped that Viv would like the dress.

Or ignore it.

One or the other.

❉ ❉ ❉

Viv clutched onto her champagne. Okay, probably it was sparkling wine, but still, she held on to it like she'd punch anyone who tried to take it away.

"Oh my, don't you look wonderful."

She forced herself to smile as Cal approached. "Thank you."

"You can unclench your teeth," Cal said. "I'm not going to bite. And you don't have to play nice with me, I promise. Are you feeling okay? The crowd not too much for you?"

"I'm fine," Viv said, rather more sharply than she meant to. Because she wasn't exactly fine. Alice wasn't here and it bothered her more than she'd thought.

"I have to thank you," said Cal, whose blue dress was sparkling in the fairy-lights dangling from the ceiling. "You handed out more invitations than anyone else. Half the people here are here because of you."

Viv managed a more genuine smile this time. It felt good to help. "We should thank you," she said. "You've made the library look magical."

The shelves were pushed back, tiny lights twinkled from every corner, a small trio was playing in the corner, and trays of glasses were being shuttled through the crowds.

"Let's just hope it's enough," Cal said in a worried tone. "I'm not sure that we're going to succeed here, this is just too short notice."

But Viv wasn't listening anymore.

Alice had arrived.

She was standing in the doorway, blonde hair piled on top of her head, a red dress that looked painted on, high heels and Viv's heart was about to explode from the sight of her.

A shock of heat shot through her core and if there had been any doubt at all about what those fizzy feelings were, it was gone now.

Viv could say absolutely and for sure that Alice was turning her on in ways she'd forgotten existed.

Fuck.

Double fuck.

Triple fuck.

She gulped down her champagne and grabbed another two glasses from the waiter passing by.

"What—" began Cal. Then she turned and saw. "Ah. I'll, um, leave you to it," she said, disappearing off into the shadows.

Viv groaned to herself, finished one of the glasses in one shot, and then turned and fled.

There was only so much she could handle at once, and Alice had pushed her way over her limit.

＊ ＊ ＊

Alice frowned as she looked around the room. She'd seen Viv, of that she was sure. She'd seen Viv in tight, ankle length trousers with high heels, a long jacket covering her behind, sparkles in her ears, hair swept back so that she looked almost like a pirate.

She was certain she'd seen her because her heart had stopped beating for a moment and she'd cursed herself for coming.

She'd spent over a week avoiding Viv's touch. A week keeping social distancing rules. A week of behaving herself and schooling her thoughts.

And then Viv showed up in an outfit like that.

She took a breath, then another, then came to a decision.

She'd find Viv, tell her that she wasn't feeling well, then she'd leave. That would be easiest. Simplest.

But first she had to find her.

In the end, it was Cal, radiant in a blue dress, that pointed Alice to the bookshelves in the corner. "I think she was feeling a little overwhelmed," Cal confided.

Alice nodded and quietly made her way over to where Viv was hiding.

The shelves had been moved, creating a little niche between two sections. Alice took a breath before she rounded the corner.

And there she was.

Eyes sparkling, mouth swollen, leaning up against the shelves like every dirty dream Alice had ever had.

Alice bit her lip and tried to force herself to feel nothing.

❊ ❊ ❊

In the end, it was a matter of a second. Less. A millisecond.

One moment, Viv was standing alone, wondering what was going on, what she was supposed to do, how she was going to deal with whatever it was that was happening inside her head, inside her body.

The next, Alice was there, appearing around the corner like a dream, and the world stopped spinning.

Because in the end, what did it matter?

Sure, there were details. Alice was very definitely female. Alice was supposed to be her life coach. Viv was straight and divorced and far older and a million other things.

But they were just that, details. Viv knew what she was feeling, knew that there was nothing wrong with those feelings, knew that they were both consenting adults and that this was as natural as kissing Bill in the front of his dad's truck.

So why did this have to be any different?

Alice bit her lip, her eyes wide and blue, and Viv was damned if she could think of any reason at all why this should be any different.

So she stepped forward, close enough that she could smell Alice's perfume.

"Viv," Alice began.

But Viv shook her head. "Not now, not right now," she murmured.

She reached out, tucking a strand of hair behind Alice's ear.

"Viv..."

She took a breath, unsure of exactly how this was supposed to go. Her head knew it should be just like any other encounter. But her heart was throbbing in her chest and making it difficult to breathe.

She just needed to do it. Like stepping off that platform at the carnival.

"I want to kiss you." There. Done. Said.

"Viv, that's really not a good idea, I think—" Alice's cheeks were flushing, her eyelashes were so long that they almost brushed her cheekbones when she looked down.

"No," said Viv again. "No excuses, no justifications. Simple question: do you want me to?"

Stillness. Silence. Viv could hear a heart beating and she didn't know if it was hers or Alice's.

Then slowly, gently, Alice nodded.

CHAPTER NINETEEN

From the second that her lips touched Alice's, Viv knew that her decision had been right. She knew that this was right. Warmth coursed through her and her stomach dropped and her knees shook and as she reached up and cupped Alice's face, she couldn't imagine a world where this didn't happen.

Slowly, carefully, she kissed her, as though she might break, or as though they might break the world by doing this wrong. And when Alice wrapped her arms around Viv's neck, Viv felt tears sparking behind her eyelids at the sheer perfection of the moment.

She tasted of cheap champagne and spearmint gum, she smelled of citrus and vanilla, she felt like the softest of blankets and Viv's heart thrummed so hard in her chest that she almost wondered if she would die right then.

Which wouldn't be the worst thing.

To go out like this, in the arms of perfection.

And something inside was pressing for more. Her hips pushed forward, making sure that her whole body was aligned with Alice's, feeling the full length of her as the warmth trickled down between her legs and her breath started to come faster.

Alice hiccuped a laugh into the kiss and the warmth grew hotter still until Viv moaned with frustration at the fact that they weren't already naked, weren't already sweating and panting and together.

And Alice pulled back.

Viv's eyes flickered open. "Was it okay? Did I do something wrong?"

Alice shook her head and smiled a little. "No, nothing wrong," she said.

"Then why—" she was already reaching out to pull Alice back into her arms.

"Viv, there are people out there."

Only then did the sounds of the fundraiser come back to her, the clinking of glasses and the chattering of people. Viv heaved a sigh and extricated herself. "Right. Yes. I forgot."

Alice's lips twitched. "Forgot?"

Viv looked down at Alice's cleavage. "That dress makes it easy to forget about a lot of things," she said.

"Viv, this—"

"—isn't the moment for all of this," Viv finished for her, even though she wasn't entirely sure that was what Alice had been going to say. "You're right. We need to go back out there."

Alice nodded and Viv desperately wanted to kiss her again. "Back to the party," Alice ordered.

Viv reached for Alice's hand, tangling their fingers together for just a moment as Alice turned to leave. "But it wasn't wrong?" she asked.

"No," Alice said. "No, it wasn't wrong." She squeezed Viv's hand and then walked away, back out to the party-goers.

Viv took a second, leaning back against the bookshelves, getting her breath back, wondering what had started, wondering what the sparkling, fizzing feeling inside her stomach was. Too much champagne maybe.

Except it wasn't.

It was excitement, she realized, as she straightened up to go back. Excitement at the start of something. And a little something extra too. Hope.

For the first time in as long as she could remember, Viv felt hope.

"A VERY SUCCESSFUL evening," Cal said, clinking her glass against Viv's. "Thank you so much again."

Viv nodded, eyes searching for Alice, loathe to stop looking at her for even a second. "You're welcome."

"Is everything alright?" the librarian asked.

Viv frowned. "Why wouldn't it be?"

"Oh, I don't know, you're dancing around like a cat on a hot tin roof, you can't take your eyes off a woman you say is just your life coach, and I'm not entirely sure that you've heard a word I've said about the auction."

"I, uh, well..." Viv stumbled, but the words wouldn't come.

Cal grinned. "You got it that bad, huh?"

"Got what?" said Viv, sharply.

Cal sniffed and sipped her champagne. "You know, once upon a time, I had the very same thing happen."

"What thing?" asked Viv, wanting to escape the conversation now.

"I met a girl at a party," said Cal. "And she was the most beautiful thing that I'd ever seen. She made my heart beat too fast, my cheeks flush too red, and made me trip over my words so badly that I could barely string a sentence together."

"I see."

"So I left the party," Cal said. "Just walked out, because who wants to feel like an idiot?"

Viv looked at her now. "You just left?"

Cal nodded. "I did. And then I heartily regretted it for days afterward."

"So what happened?"

With a wide grin, Cal nodded to where Lea was piling glasses onto a tray. "She found me. Said she'd asked everyone at the party who the weird girl who couldn't talk was until she found someone who knew my name. Then she chased me down."

Against her will, Viv laughed.

"And then, well, then I married her. Eventually."

"It was that easy, huh?" asked Viv. She could see Alice now, talking to someone in the far corner, could see the line of her delicate throat as she lifted her head to laugh.

"I wouldn't say it was easy," Cal said. "Nothing worth having is ever easy. But it was beautiful. It is beautiful. And I thank the heavens every day that she bothered to find me. Though I do have to remind myself of how lucky I am when I'm picking up wet towels off the bathroom floor. I swear, the woman doesn't know how to fold and hang."

"She's so young," Viv said, eyes still on Alice.

"She's younger than you," said Cal, following her gaze. "I wouldn't say she's so young. Alice seems like an old soul to me. Older than you, maybe even older than me."

Viv chuckled. "Yes, there is that."

"You didn't ask for my advice," said Cal. "But I'll give it anyway, because I'm an interfering old lady like that. You two have something, it's obvious to anyone who sees it. How that thing works out will be up to the two of you and will depend entirely on how well you communicate with each other. That's all a good relationship is, you know, communication."

Viv thought back to screaming arguments with Bill.

"You can't force what isn't there, but equally, I'm not entirely sure you can escape what is there, if you know what I mean? Hang on in there, stay around for the whole show, you might be surprised at the ending."

Viv opened her mouth to speak, but Cal was hurrying over to help Lea with the tray she was carrying and there was no one to speak to.

So she settled back to watch Alice instead.

In the space of one evening her life had changed.

No, that wasn't true at all.

Her life had begun changing the second that Alice had walked through her door. This was just a culmination of that. And it felt... right. Good. Exciting.

She couldn't help but smile as she watched Alice turn and walk toward her. It filled her heart up to see Alice's smile.

Not that it didn't have other effects. There was no denying the physical attraction that was there, those fizzing feelings that had suddenly become explosive.

She reached out as Alice neared her, anxious to touch her again. But Alice stepped to one side. And Viv's hope and excitement faded, replaced by a throbbing worry in her chest.

"Are you alright?"

Alice nodded, then bit her lip and Viv wanted to throw her to the ground right there. "Viv, we need to discuss all this."

"Uh, yeah, of course. It was fast, I'm sorry, maybe we should have talked first." Communication was key, according to Cal at least.

Alice smiled at that. "Maybe, but I'm not saying I regret what happened. Just that we really should talk about it. But maybe not tonight? I'm exhausted and I'm guessing you are too. Maybe we should think about things and come to the discussion with clear heads tomorrow?"

Which rather spoiled Viv's growing idea of whisking Alice home and throwing her on the bed before sliding that red dress... She took a deep breath. "Sure, of course. That makes perfect sense." Alice, so logical, so smart, so organized. "Um, so..."

Alice took her arm and some of the worry drained out of her. "Come on, why don't you walk me to my car. Cal said that she and Lea will see you home, they're on foot and live two blocks from you."

Stunned into silence by the touch of Alice's hand, Viv nodded.

The air outside was fresh and cool, the smell of cut grass lingering from the park the next block over. They walked quietly all the way to Alice's car and Viv, for once in her life, didn't know what to say.

In the end, it was Alice that stood up on tip toes and lightly kissed Viv's cheek. "Thank you," she said. "It was a magical evening."

Then she was getting in her car and driving away and Viv wanted to hope, wanted to feel that excitement again. But she had the awful feeling that she'd just been turned down in the most polite way possible.

CHAPTER TWENTY

A lice walked slowly up the building stairs, unable to keep the smile off her face.

She shouldn't be smiling.

She shouldn't have let the kiss happen.

But it had happened and it had been magical and miraculous and goddammit, she needed to get her feet back on the ground.

She could still taste Viv's lips, still feel those hips pushing insistently against hers. She lost her breath at the memory of Viv's hands cupping her face and nearly fell when she missed a stair.

Back on the ground.

Things weren't all sunshine, she reminded herself, even though Viv felt like warm, warm sunshine after a long winter. There were ethical considerations here. She couldn't be Viv's life coach and her... whatever. Lover. Kisser. Potential. It was way too early to label things.

Which meant she'd have to choose. Not the easiest decision in the world. She grinned to herself. Not the hardest either though.

She quietly slid her key into the lock and opened the front door, but light from the kitchen told her that Harrison wasn't sleeping yet, so she cried out "I'm home!" and practically danced into the kitchen.

"Aren't you glowing," Harrison said.

She meant it as a joke but it came out almost as an accusation.

Harrison's eyes were red and her hair was a mess and Alice suspected that the cup in front of her didn't just contain hot chocolate.

"Oh dear," Alice said, sliding into a chair. "What's wrong?"

"Nothing," said Harrison. She pasted on a smile. "And I didn't mean to ruin your buzz. How was the fundraiser?"

But Alice leaned forward. "Harrison, you've been crying. What happened?"

She shrugged. "Nothing, I just didn't get the damn job again and then I started to feel sorry for myself."

A crack appeared in Alice's happiness, a reminder of why she was doing this, what was at stake. She wanted nothing more than to run to Viv's house, bang on the door, and give up all thoughts of stupid life coaching.

Instead, she reached across the table and took Harrison's hand. "It's going to be alright," she said. "You're going to find something."

"I think I've applied to every pharmaceutical company in town," Harrison wailed.

Alice shook her head and got up for the tissue box on top of the refrigerator. "You haven't. I'm sure you haven't. And even if you have, they're keeping you on file and you'll get a call any day now asking you to interview for something."

Harrison had been there for her. Harrison had helped out when she needed help. Harrison, for a time, had been her only connection in town. She'd been the one to introduce her to friends, the best restaurants and bars, the one to keep her company and show her how to handle life.

Returning the favor was non-negotiable.

She sat back down at the table and forcibly pushed all thought of Viv from her mind. But that image of her in that suit, in those heels, just kept popping back up again and again.

IT WAS A sunny morning, not that the light made this any easier. She'd been up until after three with Harrison and then tossed and turned for the rest of the night.

But this needed to be done, this conversation had to happen, and it needed to be sooner rather than later.

It was, Alice thought as she climbed out of her car, a dangerous conversation to be having. She had no intention of lying, she couldn't do that, not to Viv. But she needed to keep this job, she couldn't get fired, not right now, she needed that pay check.

Being an adult sucked, she thought sourly, as she walked up the two steps to the door.

"Oh," Viv said when she opened the door. "I, uh, I wasn't... You're early and, um..."

Her cheeks had turned red and she couldn't look Alice in the eye. Which made Alice want to hold her and tell her that everything was going to be alright, which obviously, would be counter-productive at this point.

She cleared her throat. "Viv, can I come in? Can we talk?"

"Uh, yeah, sure, I, um, coffee?"

She weighed up the chances of Viv tossing the coffee at her when she said what needed to be said and decided that she'd survive it, especially if Viv continued not looking at her. "Yes, please."

Max was lapping at water in his bowl as they walked through to the kitchen. Alice pulled out a high chair from the island and sat down as Viv flicked the coffee machine on.

"We need to talk," she said. Great opener. She took a breath. "First, I, um, I don't want you to feel bad about last night. I certainly don't. It was fantastic and wonderful and I wanted what happened to happen just as much as you did."

Viv poured coffee, passed a cup over, then leaned on the counter with her elbows. "And yet I feel like I'm being dumped, why is that?" There were shadows under her eyes that looked like bruises.

Alice sighed and looked down into her cup. "Look, this isn't appropriate. I'm your life coach. I'm supposed to be here teaching you to be happy, it would be an abuse of my position to expect any more than that."

"What if kissing you is what makes me happy?" Viv countered, leaning down further.

Alice could see her cleavage, could see the roundness of the top of her breasts as she leaned and a shot of heat went through her core. She gritted her teeth. "Viv, you know what I'm saying here. You're in a vulnerable position."

"I absolutely am not, I feel better than I have in months."

"But you are. I mean, you are with me. How can I help you if we get entangled together? I know it's not illegal or forbidden or anything else, but it just doesn't seem right."

Viv looked at her long and hard, then shrugged. "Alright, then I'll fire you."

Alice blew out a breath. "Okay, I can't let that happen. Not yet. I need this job, Viv."

"You're not even a real life coach," Viv said, standing up straighter.

"I need this job," Alice said again, wanting to plead with Viv to understand.

"We're two consenting adults, I don't get why this is a big deal."

Alice rubbed at her eyes. "We're two adults, Viv. Which is why we can both recognize when something is happening at the wrong time and—"

"Wrong time?" Viv broke in. Her eyes sparkled a little. "Will there be a right time?"

"I don't know," Alice said. "I can't promise that."

But maybe there could be. All she knew was that it wasn't right now, that she couldn't get involved with Viv while she had this job, and she couldn't not have this job.

"Then I'll wait," Viv said stoutly. "I'll wait and you'll come to your senses and then, well, then we'll see what happens."

"Viv, I have to ask, are you bisexual? I had no idea, but you seem to be taking the idea of all of this awfully well."

"Never thought about it," Viv said. "And I don't really care, to be honest. What I do know is that you make me feel good and

I'd like more of feeling good. And if that means that I need to wait around until you think that I'm ready to handle an adult relationship, then I guess that's what I'll do."

Alice bit her lip. She didn't want to encourage Viv. She also didn't want to discourage her. She knew what they both wanted. She just wasn't sure how they were going to get there. "I'm not asking you to wait."

"I'm not saying that you did," countered Viv. "Now, what's on the menu for today? The sooner we get this process started and finished, the sooner you can say I'm fixed and we can go back to more important issues."

Alice frowned. "This isn't about fixing you, Viv, is that what you think?"

"Isn't it?" Viv scratched her nose. "I need fixing, I'm fine with that. I was lost. Lost and dark and I didn't know how to get back. But now I've found a path and I'm walking it. Which is thanks to you, and to Evie. As soon as I find my way completely back to the way I was before, then I'll be in a position to ask you out on a date. So let's get a move on."

"Viv—"

"No, enough chatter. You said this can't happen now, so it can't happen. Let's move on, please."

She knew that this conversation hadn't gone well, but she wasn't exactly sure why. Something was off here in the way Viv viewed herself, or the way she thought life coaching worked. But it was also a discussion that needed an ending.

If they talked any more, she had a feeling she'd talk herself right back into dating Viv.

Even the word made her stomach flip over.

So maybe this casual detente was best. Maybe they needed time and distance and things would work themselves out.

"Alright then," she said. "I think it's about time we started clearing out other rooms of the house, what do you say?"

"We can start in the bedroom," said Viv, then blushed as she realized what she'd said.

"Maybe we should start in here," said Alice.

CHAPTER
TWENTY ONE

No matter which way she looked at it, that kiss was the best thing she'd done in months. Years. Maybe ever.

Which was why Alice's distance was so frustrating.

Not that Viv had any intention of allowing Alice to hide behind excuses. If she was being turned down, then fine, she was a big girl, she could handle it. Except, whispered a little voice in the back of her head, you didn't handle it too well the last time, did you? When Bill left?

This time was different though. She'd wait it out, see how things developed. Because she had a feeling that this was just meant to be. Just like the feeling you had about Bill, whispered the voice in the back of her head.

"I don't know," Evie was saying on the phone. "Nothing too interesting, I guess. What about you?"

Viv took a breath and blew it out long and hard. "Eh, nothing new," she said.

There was a pause and the phone line crackled between them. Viv didn't know why she wasn't telling the truth, other than she didn't want to jinx things. And maybe because she was sure that Evie was keeping something from her too.

"Really?" Evie said. "Because you sound different, and I'm sensing that you're not telling me something."

Viv snorted.

"What exactly is that snort supposed to mean?"

"It means that I'm not the only one not saying something," said Viv. "You've got your dream opportunity, you're in London, and you're acting like your hamster just died or something. I've never heard you so down."

"It's... it's complicated," Evie said.

"Well, in that case, my excuse is the same. It's complicated."

"Come on, Viv, I don't mean to shut you down. You seem happy. Why don't you tell me about it?"

"Why don't you tell me why you're so depressed?"

"Because it's complicated," Evie said again.

"You know, I've told you everything since I was seven," Viv said. "And you go away and just like that, suddenly we're not confidants anymore. What's up with that?"

"Viv—"

"No, it's fine. I get it. You can't talk to me because it's complicated. I'm only trying to help. You know, in the same way that you help me, the way you have life coaches banging down my doors?"

"Viv—"

But Viv hung up. She was irritated and out of sorts and knew that she was taking it out on Evie.

"Yelling at Evie just because I'm not getting laid is pathetic," she said to Max, who just lifted an ear in response.

"It's pathetic and I should know better," she went on. Then she spotted the box by the bedroom door. "And you and I are going for a walk. Come on, lazy dog, up you get."

Maybe fresh air would make her feel better.

She clipped Max's leash on, picked up the box, balancing it on one hip, and went out through the front door.

"Afternoon," Mr. Webber said, waving from his front porch.

"Afternoon," she said back, wondering just when they'd become polite. It was a nice feeling though, she wouldn't deny that. Better than yelling at each other anyway.

"That fundraiser was great, I was glad to get out of the house.

How did it do? How much did we raise?"

Viv shrugged. "Not a clue. But I'm off to the library now, I'll ask around."

He waved her off and she and Max went on their way.

The warm sunshine and clean air lightened her mood just a little. Enough so that by the time she pushed the library door open she could smile at Cal anyway.

"I was doing a clear out," she said, depositing the box on the library counter. "There's a few books here, I thought you could add them to the pile for the book sale."

"Every little bit helps," Cal said, pulling the box toward her. "And how are you this fine morning? Get things sorted out with Alice?"

"Are you always quite so direct?"

Cal's eyes twinkled. "Aren't you?" she asked. "And from that I take it that things aren't going well in paradise?"

Viv harrumphed and Cal laughed.

"Things will work out, just you wait and see."

"How are you so sure about that?" Viv asked suspiciously.

"If you don't have hope, what else is there?" Cal responded. "And everything generally does work out in the end. Maybe not the way you'd have expected, but an ending comes around eventually."

"If you're not careful, I'll take the title of Little Miss Sunshine away from Alice and give it to you instead," Viv grumbled.

"I can't say that I'd mind that. What's the problem, anyway?"

"She's my life coach," Viv said. "So she can't be anything else."

"So, fire her," Cal suggested.

"She needs the job."

Cal rolled her eyes behind her glasses. "Then find her a new job. Honestly, young people nowadays. You know you're supposed to fight for love, right?"

"I can't just go around finding jobs for people!"

"You can suggest the idea. You can be proactive," Cal said. "Or you can just wait around hoping that she'll change her mind. You can be a problem maker or a problem solver, it's up to you."

"Jesus, you sound like Evie."

"Who's Evie exactly?"

Viv explained. And then she found herself explaining about London and about Evie's strange phone calls and that led back to Evie hiring Alice and then to Bill, and before she knew it, an hour had passed and Cal was handing her a coffee in the library office.

"Sounds like you've been through the wars," Cal said.

Viv shrugged. "No more than anyone else, I guess."

"It also sounds like you have trouble asking for help," said Cal. "I mean, I'm no expert, but from what you say, you keep things bottled up. That's no good. There's nothing wrong with asking for help, you know."

Viv scowled at her. "Asking for help? Communicating? That's your thing, right."

"Hey, I'm a librarian, words are my thing. And has it occurred to you that by opening up yourself, you might encourage others to open up. Like your friend Evie, for example?"

"I suppose."

"And now you're grumpy because I'm right and you hate other people being right."

"I hate other people telling me what to do."

"Except Alice," Cal said.

"Huh?"

"Except Alice," Cal repeated. "She tells you what to do all the time and you don't seem to mind that."

"She's different."

"That she is," said Cal. "I stand by what I said though, communication is key to most things in life. And things will work out eventually."

"Maybe you should be my life coach instead," Viv said, draining her coffee cup.

"Alice needs the job," said Cal. "But you're welcome here any time for a chat. At least as long as we're here."

"What's that supposed to mean?"

A look of sadness flitted across Cal's face. "The fundraiser was great, and we're still trying, but I'm not sure we're going to be saving this place, Viv. It might be time to face facts."

"No, don't give up. Giving up is for quitters."

"Sometimes, giving up is for realists," said Cal. "But I'll fight. For now anyway. And you'd better get back to Max, his shady nap patch outside is about to turn into a sun trap and we don't want him to get heat stroke."

So Viv and Max wandered home, Max thinking about dinner and Viv thinking about just how exactly she was going to communicate better and solve her problems with Evie and Alice both. But somehow, just knowing that Cal was on her side made things seem a little better, a little more hopeful.

She was rounding the corner when she saw the car parked in front of her house. It was unfamiliar, and she hurried a little, wanting to know who was there. Probably no one, she guessed, probably someone for the neighbors.

But when she got closer, she could see a man standing in front of her door.

"Hey," he shouted, waving to her as he saw her.

Webber stood up on his porch. "He's been waiting over there a while now. Everything okay? You want me to call anyone?"

Viv hesitated but shook her head. "No, no, it's alright," she said, even though she was far from sure.

She started down her driveway. "Why are you here?"

"Where is she?"

And Viv frowned. "What do you mean?"

"Where's Evie? Where's my wife?" Greg said.

Max barked and Viv came in closer. "Wait, you don't know where she is?"

And the look in Greg's eyes as he shook his head was almost heart-breaking.

CHAPTER
TWENTY TWO

V iv put a mug of coffee in front of Greg and leaned on the kitchen counter. "Tell me what happened."

He shook his head. "I have no idea what happened. She just walked out. She left."

"That doesn't sound like Evie," said Viv.

He shrugged. "What can I tell you? I came home from work and she wasn't there. Some of her stuff still is, but a lot is gone too."

She wanted to believe him. She remembered how she'd felt the day she'd walked into a half-empty house. And Bill was an asshole, she should have been glad to be rid of him. But that didn't stop the sick feeling, the feeling of betrayal, the terrifying feeling of suddenly facing life alone again.

"But you've waited over two weeks to come and find me," she said.

His eyes flared. "So you did know she was gone?"

"I did," she sighed. "I didn't know that you didn't know, if that's any help at all. Why wait so long?"

"I thought that maybe she needed space or something, I don't know. Maybe there was a business trip I forgot about. Something like that."

"Really?" Viv asked, remembering why the two of them had

never been so close. "Or were you just busy with your own things and work was more important? You figured she'd come back eventually."

He turned the coffee mug in his hands. "I'm here now," he said softly. "I know we don't always see eye to eye, I know I should have tried harder sooner, but even you can't say that I don't love my wife." He looked up at her with sad, dark eyes. "Viv, do you know where she is?"

Now she was torn. Half of her wanted to rescue him from his uncertainty because she'd been in his position, and because he was right. She knew he adored Evie. The other half of her needed to side solidly with Evie. She was her best friend. If Evie had left, there was a reason for leaving.

Which went a long way to explaining why Evie was so strange on the phone.

"I know where she is," she said eventually.

Greg's face lit up.

"But I'm not going to tell you," she finished.

"She's my wife."

"She's an independent person with her own wants and needs, she's not your property," Viv barked. Then she took a breath. "I get that you're worried. She won't answer your calls?"

Greg shook his head. "I've tried a thousand times."

"Then I'll talk to her," said Viv. "I'll tell her you're worried and that she needs to check in with you, at least tell you what's going on. Okay?"

"Is she okay?" Greg asked.

Viv considered this. "Yes," she said. "She's okay. Not great, but okay. She's not injured or anything, if that's what you're worried about."

Greg swallowed but nodded. "Right then. You have my number?"

Viv vaguely recalled adding him to her phone. "I'll call you when I get in touch with her. But it'll probably be tomorrow or the next day."

He stood up, leaving his mug on the counter. "Thank you," he said quietly.

Viv showed him out of the house, closing the door behind him, then leaned back against the door. What the hell was all this? What was going on?

The fact that Evie would leave Greg was hard enough to believe. They were generally sickeningly in love, the kind of couple that kissed goodbye before going to the bathroom. But the fact that Evie wouldn't tell her about it, that was what really hurt.

She locked the front door and grabbed her phone from the bedroom. Time to get to the bottom of this, whatever it was.

TWENTY THREE TIMES. That was how many times she'd called. By the time it was morning and she'd walked Max and was showered and dressed and sitting on her bed ready to make call number twenty four, she was thinking that Evie was screening her calls.

Or maybe something had happened to her. A shiver went through her as she pressed the call button.

The doorbell rang and she glanced toward the shadow outside then checked the time. Fuck. Alice. Another thing she needed to deal with. One thing at a time.

"Come on in," she yelled. "It's open."

She heard the sound of the door opening over the tinny ring of the phone in her ear. She growled as she put the phone down. Evie was ignoring her, that much was clear. She ended the call, flung the phone on the bed, turned and shrieked.

"Who the hell are you?" she fumbled to get her phone back. "I'm calling the police, I'm warning you."

"Hold on, hold on," said the man. He was standing in the hallway, pale and plump, with a distinct widow's peak. "I'm your life coach. Foster Davison?"

She was already dialing, but managed to stop herself before putting in the final digit. She scowled up at him. The name was familiar. "You're supposed to be in hospital."

"I was in hospital." He raised an eyebrow at her. "Want to see my scar?"

"Where do you go around just letting yourself into other people's houses?"

"You were the one that yelled to come in," he said, reasonably.

"Because I thought you were Alice." Ah. Alice. Her heart started to beat faster. Was that what this was about? Alice wasn't here. Alice had dumped her. Alice had sent her sick boss in her place. Viv could feel sweat collecting at the back of her neck.

"Mmm, Alice," Davison said, as though he didn't quite approve of her. He looked around the house, craning his neck to see in the different rooms from the hallway. "I would have expected a cleaner and more orderly home by this point in the process."

And despite the growing fear that Alice wasn't coming, that Alice had ditched her, she couldn't help but grit her teeth. "Alice has done a fine job. An excellent job." Because that was the truth, whether Alice had lost her nerve and refused to face her or not.

"Alice?" Davison said, still looking around the house. "Well, I'm here now, so no more need to worry."

"You're here?" Viv took a breath. "I don't want you here. I was doing just fine with Alice."

"But Alice isn't even a real life coach," he said, then a look flashed over his face as he realized what he was admitting to. "Yet," he added.

"I don't care. I'd prefer to work with Alice. Otherwise I'll fire the both of you." There. See what Alice did with that. She said she needed the job.

Davison took a step toward the bedroom. "But she's not a real life coach."

"No, she's an assistant."

"Yes, but a personal assistant. As in my secretary. Not as in 'assistant life coach.'"

The news took Viv off guard. A personal assistant. Had Alice lied? She wracked her brains trying to remember. Had she lied or had Viv assumed? She licked her dry lips.

It was too much. Too much was happening at one time. And

Foster Davison was taking another step toward the bedroom.

Evie had left her husband and was avoiding her calls. Alice hadn't shown up and someone else had instead. Maybe Alice had bent the truth a little about what her role was. But overwhelmingly, Viv's feeling was one of being alone.

Alone with a man she didn't know approaching her bedroom.

"Get out."

Davison stopped. "I'm sorry?"

"Get out," she spat. "Out of here. Out of my house."

"We have a contract," Davison began. "And I can help you, Vivien. That's what I'm here for."

"No. Get out of here. You're fired."

"You don't mean that."

She was up, on her feet, going to the window and opening it, praying that Mr. Webber was on his porch. "Get out," she said to Davison, who was coming closer.

"Come now, Vivien, let us talk and—"

But she was already shouting, calling for Webber, who sprang down off his porch when he heard her.

She backed away from the window, hearing Webber crashing toward the door, opening it, standing in the hallway and huffing, taking in the situation.

"I'd like this man to leave," she said, her voice shaky.

She didn't calm down until Davison was safely out of the house and Webber had checked on her and gone back to his porch.

Only then did she sit back on the bed and start to cry.

Things had been going so well, she'd felt so strong, and now, now she felt like things were crumbling. But the thing that bothered her most was Alice. Why hadn't Alice come? Why had Alice left her like this?

She felt shaky inside. There had to be a reason. She was just too tired, too wrong-footed to put things together.

Because she trusted Alice.

Didn't she?

CHAPTER TWENTY THREE

Alice rang the doorbell, peered through the glass, and then rang again. It took two more rings and one knock before she saw movement inside.

"What?" the voice came through the door.

"Viv? It's me, Alice. Can I come in?"

There was a long pause. Long enough that Alice wondered whether she'd be allowed in at all. Then the door opened.

"What happened?" Alice said, seeing the paleness in Viv's face.

"What happened? Why are you asking me? You're the one that didn't damn well show up."

"You had Foster Davison escorted out of your house," Alice said, still reeling from the explosion that Foster had had once he'd walked into the office. She'd had a thorough dressing down, with everything she'd done questioned.

And then, Foster had calmed down and told her to get back to Viv's and get the contract running again. Which Alice wasn't entirely sure she wanted to do now that she saw Viv's face.

Viv scowled, but the door opened a little further until finally it was fully open and Viv was walking into the living room and Alice was closing the door and following her.

"Viv, don't be angry with me, please."

"A strange man appears in my home and I'm not supposed to

be angry?" Viv said. "He wouldn't leave. I told him no and he wouldn't go."

Alice took a breath. "Viv, I had no idea. Please. Let me explain."

Viv slouched into the armchair and Alice perched on the edge of the couch.

"I got a call this morning from Foster. He told me to go to the office and I figured he was meeting me there, so I went. I tried to call you, twice, but your phone was busy."

Viv blushed a little.

"So then I thought that I probably wouldn't be too late, maybe a half hour or so and that you were obviously busy anyhow, and you could always call me if you needed me."

"You didn't know he'd be here?"

"The next thing I know, Foster is storming into the office yelling that you've thrown him out, that you've fired him, that I've ruined this contract and have thrown away all his hard work in building this company."

"Fucker."

Alice was startled by the word, but then she smiled a little. "Yeah, that's one way of putting it. He's... difficult."

"He's an asshole," Viv said.

"He is, but he's my boss and I need this job. At least right now." Alice rubbed at her nose and decided that the whole truth was necessary. "He's sent me here to persuade you to go ahead with the coaching."

"I don't know," said Viv.

"You were doing so well. You are doing so well." Alice couldn't force this on her. "But I understand if you don't want to continue. Perhaps you should think about continuing with another company."

Viv was shaking her head. "You know what I was afraid of?" she asked.

"Foster?"

"Yes, kind of. But mostly I was afraid that you'd gone, that you'd left and you couldn't handle being close to me anymore and that I'd never see you again. That's why I panicked, that's why I lost it, I..." She trailed off and blinked away what Alice suspected were tears.

"Viv..." Alice scooted up the couch until she could put a hand on Viv's knee.

"But then I had time to think, to think about everything, and I think you're wrong."

"Wrong?" The hand on the knee maybe wasn't the best idea. Alice could feel warmth flowing up her arm and into her core, she could smell Viv's perfume and suddenly the picture was there. Suddenly, she was back in the library, pushing Viv back up against the bookshelves as their lips met and her breath was speeding up.

"Alice, what if you're what I needed?"

"Huh?" She was trying to control herself, trying not to look at Viv's breasts, almost visible through a white shirt.

"Alice, look at me."

Obediently, she looked up.

"Your job was to teach me to be happy. You make me happy. I don't know why it took so long to find you, or why it took me so long to realize, but you do. You said this coaching business wasn't about fixing me, and maybe you were right about that."

"I was?" Alice said, mesmerized by her lips.

"Maybe this wasn't about getting the old me back. Maybe the old me is gone and the reason I couldn't do anything, couldn't go out or meet new people or anything else was because I kept looking for the old me. When what I really needed was to find a new me, a better one, a wiser one."

Alice reached out for her hand. "I think that's the smartest thing I've heard you say."

Viv snorted. "Seriously? I swear I get smarter than that. I'm not as dumb as you might think I am."

"I don't think you're dumb."

"The point is, Alice, I like you. I like you a lot. You're the first person I've liked in a long time. And the thought of you not being there scared me. So I lashed out. Which was dumb, I'll admit that. Even more to the point, I think you like me too, or am I wrong?"

Alice closed her eyes for a moment. "No, you're not wrong."

"I know, I know, but you're my life coach and blah, blah, blah. Except you're not."

Alice's eyes flashed open again. "I'm not." It wasn't a question. It was a statement of a fact that she'd only just realized the truth of.

"Even if I re-hire the company, sleazy Davison will be doing the coaching, you're his personal assistant. Which I didn't know about, by the way. When you said assistant, I assumed you meant assistant coach."

"Like football?"

Viv nodded.

"Crap. I'm sorry, Viv, I didn't think, I..."

"Alice, we're having a moment here, don't interrupt it."

Viv was looking at her, face stern and Alice shut her mouth.

"All of this was a lot of misunderstandings and some bad communication. Which is stupid. And I'm too old to be stupid. Alice, I want to kiss you."

"I—"

"And I want more than that. We're both adults, there's little conflict of interest at this point, and I'm damned if I'm missing out on getting laid for the first time in years because of Foster fucking Davison."

"Getting laid?" Her stomach was tumbling, flipping, her lungs refusing to inflate properly, and Viv's hand was gripping at hers and her heart was flitting in her chest like a bird. "Was getting laid on the table?"

Viv laughed. "Damn straight it is. Unless that's something you don't want?"

Alice found herself shaking her head, then nodding, then confused. "No, I mean, yes, I mean..."

But Viv was already leaning in, putting one finger under Alice's chin, tilting her face up and angling her head. Then those lips were on hers and Alice couldn't see straight, couldn't think straight. All she could do was let it happen, let her body respond to something she'd wanted so much she hadn't dared think about it.

When Viv drew back, one eyebrow was arched. "What do you say, Little Miss Sunshine? You're not my coach anymore, so that's no excuse."

"It's not," Alice admitted.

"And we both want this."

"We do." Her voice was getting huskier.

"And you're good for me," Viv said, taking her hand and pulling her up.

"I am." Again it wasn't a question.

Then Viv was taking her in her arms, pulling her in, and the kissing was happening again and the last reservation left her body.

She couldn't stop this. She had no intention of it. But she was sure it would be physically impossible to stop anyway. She tangled her fingers in Viv's hair and began to kiss her in earnest, pushing herself against Viv, wanting to feel every inch of her.

Viv put a hand on her waist, drawing her in and Alice groaned, feeling herself get wet as Viv slid that same hand under the tail of her shirt.

Viv pulled back again. "Last chance, Little Miss Sunshine. You in for the win, or you truly don't want this?"

Those deep blue eyes were boring into her and Alice felt her heart skip a bit. "You know, if you call me Little Miss Sunshine in bed, I'll be forced to get up and leave," she said.

"Ah," said Viv, voice deep. "That implies that we are going to bed."

Alice glanced around. "It's eleven o'clock in the morning."

Viv laughed. "Oh child, you have a lot to learn. Don't tell me you only think sex happens at night?"

Alice could feel herself blushing as she let Viv lead her out of the living room and across the hall. "No, that's not what I think."

"Then stop thinking about anything else except this," said Viv as they finally reached the bedroom.

"Except what?" Alice grumbled, her heart beating in her

throat and every atom of her crying out to be touched again.

"This," Viv said, pulling her in and kissing her again.

CHAPTER TWENTY FOUR

P art of it was relief that Alice had come back, that she hadn't abandoned her, that it was all a misunderstanding. But the bigger part of it was far more than that. It was something that had been building up over the days and weeks until Viv couldn't deny it anymore. It was the part of her that wanted to throw Alice on the bed and take her, the part of her that knew, just knew, that this was what she'd needed all along.

Alice's hands were moving up her spine and Viv purred in contentment before lowering her head and concentrating on the curve of Alice's smooth neck. Her fingers were already busy, unbuttoning Alice's blouse without even looking.

She drank in the scent of her, the fragility and smoothness of her, as her hands moved lower and found the zipper to Alice's skirt, then she pulled back, yanking off her own shirt at the same time.

"Hey, slow down, Little Miss Excited," Alice said, grinning. She was standing with her skirt puddled around her feet, her blouse open, a white set of matching underwear the only thing completely covering her.

Viv growled. "Excited, my ass. Get that shirt off." She reached out for it, brushing it off Alice's shoulders.

"My shirt in return for your jeans," said Alice, grinning.

Viv nearly fell over in an attempt to hurriedly pull off her jeans.

Then she thought, to hell with it, and pulled off her underwear and sports bra as well. Because she didn't want to wait and she certainly didn't want anything to come between her and Alice.

"Aren't we in a hurry?" asked Alice.

Viv reached for her, but Alice danced back. Another growl, and Viv caught her, her hands on her upper arms. "Don't make me wait any longer for you." It was half an order and half a desperate plea.

She couldn't remember feeling so turned on before, she couldn't remember wanting someone so much she could taste it. And there was Alice, skin pale in the sunlight, curves waiting to be touched, secrets waiting to be uncovered, and she couldn't wait.

"I won't make you wait," Alice said, taking a step in. "Lie down."

Viv was reaching around, attempting to unfasten Alice's bra.

"I said lie down," Alice repeated, voice stronger and harsher.

Viv shivered in anticipation and did as she was told. Alice came to lie beside her, their bodies only an inch or so apart. Close enough that Viv could feel the heat emanating from her.

"It's my turn," Alice said, more softly. "Are you sure you want this, Viv? Sure you're ready?"

In response, Viv reached out, pulled Alice toward her so that they were finally touching, so that she could feel the softness and heat of the skin. Her hands brushed down over Alice's hips, thumbs caressing her hipbones. Alice smiled and unhooked her bra and Viv gasped.

"I have no idea what I'm doing," Viv said, cautiously.

"You'll probably figure it out," said Alice, bending to kiss her collarbone, then working her way down to a nipple.

"You are a coach. Well, almost," said Viv, voice breaking into a squeak as Alice's tongue found her nipple.

"Then watch and learn," Alice said, looking up with darkened blue eyes.

As if she had a choice. Viv couldn't tear her eyes from Alice's blonde head bobbing over first one breast, then the other.

Her skin felt electric, her breath coming faster as Alice continued on her downward journey. Viv gulped, unsure for the first time. As if sensing this, Alice's hands came up, fingers entangling with Viv's as her head moved even lower.

She'd never really liked this. Not with Bill anyway. But as Alice's breath began to tickle her thighs she felt a rush of wetness. Her legs parted without much thought, and then Alice was there, her tongue gently lapping around the edges of her sex and Viv squeezed her hands tight.

"Jesus fucking Christ."

She felt a puff of laughter rather than heard it. And Alice's tongue started to move a little faster. Viv groaned, pulling her hands away so that she could grab the pillow behind her, squeezing ever harder as Alice started to circle around her clit.

"Jesus," she said again, incapable of any other kind of speech.

Then Alice's hands were between her legs, fingers were stroking her entrance, pushing against it even as her tongue moved faster.

Viv squeezed her eyes tight shut, sure she was about to lose it at any second, caught between the sensation of too much stimulation and not enough.

Alice's fingers slid inside her, filling her up and she felt her muscles squeeze against them.

Then she decided to stop thinking, stop analyzing.

Her pulse sky rocketed, her stomach clenched, she pushed her hips up to meet Alice's mouth, she wanted more and more and more until in the space of a moment she began to fly, to soar high above everything, to see nothing, hear nothing, taste nothing, only to feel the deep beating within herself.

Alice waited, staying still until she was done, then pushed up, wriggling until she was sitting astride Viv. "So?"

Viv snorted. "So, I'd say that you've got talents that aren't being thoroughly utilized in your capacity as a life coach."

Alice raised one eyebrow. "I try."

"And you're very calm and collected for someone in the midst of passion," Viv said, her hand sneaking up over the curve of Alice's waist until she could pinch at a nipple.

She could see Alice gulp, see her breath hitch in her chest.

"Too calm and collected, I'd say," she continued, letting her other hand join the first until both breasts were being caressed.

"Really?" Alice said, but her cheeks were flushed and her breath was coming faster.

"Mmm-hmm," Viv said.

In one fluid motion, she turned so that Alice fell to the bed next to her. Propping up her head on one hand she watched Alice's face as her other hand scooted down over her belly, stroked against wiry curls.

Alice's eyes were half-closed, her lips swollen and Viv's pulse was starting to beat harder again. She let her hand drift further down until Alice's legs opened for her. She paused for only a second, wanting to see the need on Alice's face, before she found the silky wetness that took her breath away again.

Then there was nothing else but the smell and sound and sight of Alice.

"I DO HAVE a job, you know," Alice said lazily, one finger hooking back a strand of Viv's hair.

"As far as you know, you do," Viv said, letting her hand rest in the curve of Alice's waist. "I mean, asshole might have fired you already."

"Eugh, don't say that."

Viv sighed. "I'll hire him back if you want. At least until you can find something else."

"No, you don't have to do that."

"I know I don't have to. In fact, since it's Evie who hired him I'm not sure I'm even qualified to fire him." She looked down into Alice's face, remembering what Cal had said about helping solve problems, not create them. "You know, you're very good at this."

Alice's lips curved into a smile. "Ready to go again?"

Viv laughed. "Not what I meant, though you're good in bed, I swear. I meant you're a great life coach. You're empathetic, orderly, logical, you seem to know what people need. Why don't you go into business for yourself?"

Alice shrugged and shuffled so that she was more comfortable against Viv's side. "I don't know. I don't know what I want, to be truthful."

"Seriously?" Viv asked. "What did you want to be when you were a kid?"

"You'll laugh."

"I won't. Promise."

"A wife."

Viv moved back a little. "For real? A wife? You know that isn't a career choice, right?"

"Yes," Alice said. "I'm beginning to realize that. But you asked. And that's the only thing I ever saw myself as."

"There's nothing wrong with being married, I suppose. Though I'm not the person to be asking about that. But you've got to have something. You can't build your idea of who you are around another person."

"Is that what you did?"

The question was an obvious one, one that she should have expected. One that she'd never answered honestly until now. Viv nodded. "I guess. I had this idea of how life should be, how it would be, I had boxes to check off a checklist and then, suddenly, everything changed. Nothing, no one was what I expected and... And it made me forget who I was."

Alice stroked her cheek. "Want to know something weird?"

"Sure."

"I imagine being married to everyone. Really. It's just a thing I do, like a mental tick. Except you. You were the exception for me."

"You never imagined yourself married to me?" It hurt more than it should. She didn't want to be married again. So why should she care what the hell Alice imagined?

THE LIFE COACH

"No," Alice said.

And she was about to say more when the knock came.

"Fuck," Viv said. "Ignore it, it'll be no one, they'll go away."

But the knock continued.

"Maybe we should get up," Alice whispered.

"Open up," came the voice from outside.

Viv sat bolt upright."Evie?"

"Let me in!"

CHAPTER
TWENTY FIVE

"Y ou're in London," Viv said, cracking the door open.

"Quite obviously, I'm not," said Evie.

"But I don't understand. Why are you here?" From the corner of her eye she could see Alice straightening the bed up.

"Because I'm not in London."

"But... how?"

"There's this thing called a plane," said Evie, pushing through the door.

Viv had no choice but to step back or get squashed. The door opened, Evie came in, Alice froze in the middle of picking up a pillow and Viv closed her eyes.

"What..." Evie began. Then she turned to Viv. "Viv?"

"Uh..."

"Hi, I'm Alice," Alice said, taking charge with a smile and hustling over to hold out her hand. "I'm Viv's life coach and you must be Evie. I've heard so much about you."

"I wish I could say the same," Evie said, looking from Alice to Viv and back again. "But there must be some mistake here. You're not Foster Davison. Plus, I'm fairly sure that screwing clients isn't on Davison's list of services."

"Screwing?" Viv said.

Evie rolled her eyes. "Viv, I've known you for a million years, so I certainly wasn't born yesterday, it's pretty damn obvious what was going on here even though I'm way too jet-lagged to make all the pieces fit properly."

Viv rubbed at her face. Too much. It was all getting to be too much again. She was starting to feel overwhelmed and slightly panicky.

Until Alice put a hand on her arm. "I think I should leave you to it," she said softly.

Viv nodded mutely.

"I'll call you, or text, later, okay?"

Again, Viv nodded.

"Evie, it was lovely to finally meet you in person," Alice said politely. Then she slipped out of the still open door, leaving Viv and Evie alone.

"What the hell was that?" Evie said.

Viv rubbed her face one more time. "Is it too early to drink?"

"Yes," Evie said. She closed the front door, deposited her purse on the hallway table, then pulled Viv in for a hug. "I'm sorry, that wasn't the welcome that I'd planned."

For a second, Viv let herself be hugged, then she pulled away. "What are you doing here?"

"How about some coffee? I think we need to talk, Viv."

"No shit, you know that Greg is looking for you, right?"

"I know that I had about a thousand missed calls from the two of you," Evie said.

It was clear from the paleness of her face, from the way her eyes were swollen, that all was not well. Viv took a deep breath, then nodded. "Come on, let's make some coffee and both spill our secrets. Deal?"

"Deal," Evie said, sounding relieved.

MAX WHIMPERED IN his sleep under the coffee table. "It wasn't really her fault," Viv said. "I mean, Davison got sick and she stepped in. And to be honest, Evie, she's done a fantastic job,

I swear it."

"And yet it's totally not what I'm paying for," Evie said, curled up in a corner of the couch. "Davison is supposed to be one of the best. He's certainly one of the most expensive. I chose him for a reason."

"Because you want me to find the old me again," said Viv. "I get it. But you weren't here, Evie. Alice has been amazing. I've been going out, talking to people, getting involved. I've been feeling better than I have in months."

A flicker of shadow went across the living room window. "Those kids are on your lawn again," Evie said idly.

"It's fine." Evie looked at her and she blushed. "I've made peace with Mr. Webber."

Evie raised an eyebrow. "Alice's work?"

Viv nodded.

"It still doesn't feel right, Viv. I'm sorry. I've got no problem with you liking women, I swear. But this... She's supposed to be helping you, you're in a vulnerable state, and you know nothing about her. Absolutely nothing. She could be married, she could be a scam artist, she could be anyone. You've known her for all of, what, a couple of weeks?"

"Three," Viv said, feeling a little sick now that she thought of it. Three weeks did seem awfully fast. But then, the last three weeks also seemed like a pivot-point, a complete change in her life, one that she'd needed and wanted.

"See? Three weeks. That's nothing, Viv. That's not long enough to change your entire life."

"You wanted me to change my life," Viv pointed out. "That was the whole point of this. And things happen, Evie. Even in just three weeks. Didn't you fall in love with Greg at a wedding? That took all of three hours."

"It's not the same thing," Evie said, but a knock on the door interrupted her. "If that's Greg," she began.

"Then I'll pretend that I've never heard your name," said Viv, getting up and slightly relieved to be leaving this conversation.

Evie wasn't wrong. It was just that Viv was more right. Evie hadn't been there, she hadn't experienced this, she hadn't seen things. She was being protective, that was all. Still though, the conversation was making Viv feel shaky.

Not what she needed after this morning.

She should be basking in the after-glow, tangled in sheets and Alice's arms. She felt a shudder of warmth go through her at the memory, so she was smiling when she opened the door.

"Mr. Webber," she said in surprise, then collected herself. "If it's about the kids, it's fine, I saw them in the garden, really—"

"No, no, it's not that. Partly I wanted to check up on you, make sure you were alright after that man coming in like that."

Strangely, she'd almost forgotten about Foster Davison in her house. "I'm fine," she said with a grin.

"Good, glad to hear it. And don't hesitate to shout out if there's something you need. But I also wanted to tell you that I took the kids to the library this morning. Bad news, I'm afraid. They'll be closing by the end of the month."

"Oh," Viv said, taking a step back. "Oh, that's awful."

Webber shrugged. "We did what we could. I suppose not every story has a happy ending."

Viv bit her lip. "Yeah, maybe not. Thanks for dropping by though."

She closed the door. Not every story had a happy ending. Why did it feel like the world was suddenly crumbling around her?

One morning with Alice. One perfect, lovely, amazing morning. And it was starting to feel like she'd tipped the world over.

"Jesus, sleep with one woman and suddenly everything else is topsy-turvy," she whispered to herself. Which was ridiculous. As though she impacted the entire rest of the world.

She strode back into the living room. "Enough about me," she said, sitting back down in the armchair.

"Was that really Webber?" Evie asked.

"It was," allowed Viv. "But enough about me, I mean it. I spilled my secrets. Now it's time you spilled yours."

Evie sighed. "Look, I came back because... Because everything isn't what I expected it to be. Because I thought going to London would make things easier, but it didn't. And because you were being weird and I thought maybe you needed me. And, a little bit, because Greg kept calling and I kept not answering."

"Why not?" Viv asked.

"I didn't know what to say to him."

Viv crossed her legs. She's known Evie for so long that sometimes she thought she knew her face better than she knew her own.

"You love Greg," she said.

Evie looked into her coffee cup.

"No, come on, don't be like that. You love him, I can see it even now. Just mentioning his name makes you lighter, makes you relax a little. You can't deny it."

"Fine," Evie huffed. "I love him. Satisfied?"

"And yet you run off to London without even telling him that you're going?"

Evie went back to staring into her coffee.

"Aren't we communicative this afternoon?" Viv said, sighing. "I can't believe you came all this way to look at a coffee cup."

Her eyes narrowed as she thought of something.

"No, that's the wrong way of thinking about things," she muttered. "The question isn't why did you come back, it's why did you go in the first place."

Evie looked up at this.

"Evie, why did you go to London? I know it was your dream, I know you wanted to go, but there's more to it than that, isn't there?"

Evie nodded.

"So?" Viv asked, starting to get impatient. "Why did you go?"

There was a long moment of silence before Evie answered. Viv could hear Webber's grandkids playing outside.

"Because I'm pregnant," Evie said, finally.

CHAPTER TWENTY SIX

Alice felt strange sitting behind a desk.

Three weeks of working with Viv and suddenly, all her real assistant skills seemed to have vanished.

Her weird feelings weren't at all helped by the fact that Foster Davison was locked into his office and she hadn't heard a word out of him since she'd arrived.

It had seemed the politic thing to do. Viv and Evie obviously had things to sort out between the two of them. Foster was back at work. She couldn't just run away home, so she'd come here. Except now she was rather wishing she hadn't.

Her computer screen flickered and switched off, just as a reminder that she hadn't actually done any work on it since she'd switched it on. She sighed.

She should be feeling great.

Thinking about Viv, she did. She felt warm and cozy and just... right inside. She might not have started out thinking of Viv as wife material, but she'd changed her mind pretty damn fast.

Which was part of the problem.

Problems that seemed all the more pressing now that she'd given in to her urges and done what she'd been wanting to do for weeks now.

Which was not how it was supposed to work.

Get the girl and everything else is supposed to fall into place, right? And yet she had a terrible feeling that that wasn't what was about to happen. She felt like one of those bugs that senses an earthquake coming and runs away.

To be clear, her morning with Viv had been absolutely consensual. She could not and would not regret it.

Except there were going to be consequences. She could feel it. She couldn't shake the feeling that as perfect as things had felt when she was in Viv's arms, the world wasn't quite ready to handle that perfection yet.

The tipping point came at four o'clock almost exactly. Alice was just thinking about leaving the office, since Foster still hadn't made an appearance, and wondering whether she dare call Viv yet, when she heard arguing coming from the corridor.

Curious, she stuck her head out of the office door to see the normally cool, collected receptionist practically running after a stormy-faced Evie.

Crap.

Alice took a step into the corridor. "It's fine," she called out. "It's all okay, I'll take things from here."

The receptionist shot her a look of relief and immediately turned in the opposite direction.

"Please," Alice said to Evie. "Come this way."

As she ushered Evie into her office and into a chair, her stomach clenched. This, she guessed, would be consequence number one.

"What can I do for you?" she asked politely, sitting down.

Evie raised one imperious eyebrow. "Are you shitting me?"

"Huh? What? No, or I don't think so," Alice said, confused.

"Listen, I've got your number. I don't know who you think you are, but there's one thing that you're not, and that's a life coach. I signed a contract with this company and, frankly, I'm seriously considering suing."

Alice gulped. "I, uh…" What could she say to that?

"Not that that's your business," Evie said with a sniff. "From what I hear, you had little choice in the matter. But it is something I'll be taking up with your idiot boss. No, my issue with you is a damn sight more personal."

"Viv," Alice said, with a sigh.

"You take a vulnerable woman and take advantage of her," Evie said. "How is that ethical? Though I suppose I should think nothing better of someone who isn't even qualified to do her job."

Which was about when Alice's patience finally wore thin.

"No."

"No?" Evie asked, looking surprised.

"No," said Alice. "I'll take the blame for a lot of things. And maybe you're right, maybe Viv and I shouldn't have done anything, maybe we should have waited. But you listen up and you listen good, your best friend is starting to find herself, she's smiling, going out, meeting people. Don't you tell me how unqualified I am to do a job that doesn't even require a qualification."

Evie stared at her.

"I'm tired of this. Everyone seems to think that Viv should go back to being her old self, but no one's actually asked her if that's what she wants to be. She thinks that she needs to be fixed, which is ridiculous. She's obviously been through a lot, been depressed, and now she's finally making a new start, finding something new, and you're here, her best friend, complaining that I don't know how to do my job."

"Hold on a second there," began Evie.

"No, you hold on," Alice said, astonished at herself, surprised that she was standing up for herself. "Viv doesn't need to go back to her old self, she needs to find something new, and I was helping her do that, whether I was 'qualified' or not. Go ahead and deny that. Deny that she looks happier, feels happier than when you left."

Evie let out a breath. "Okay, fine, you're right. She's... changed. Different. But that doesn't make what happened after any more okay. Sleeping with a client? Really? Someone who's recovering from a broken marriage?"

"Do you think that I didn't tell her all those things?" Alice said. "Of course I did. And not that it's really your business, but I was no longer her coach as of this morning."

Evie shook her head. "Think what you like, but I'm entitled to my opinion. I think you crossed a line. But that's between you and Viv, you're right it's not my business." She sighed and Alice realized just how tired she looked. "I get protective of Viv. She's so grumpy but only because she's trying to cover up how much things hurt."

"I get that," Alice said, more quietly. "I really do."

"She's special to me."

And Alice had the niggling feeling that there was something wrong, that Evie was hiding something. "It must have been hard to leave her to go to London."

"It was," Evie said, looking down at her hands. "It was also stupid. I made a spur of the moment decision and now I realize just how stupid I've been and I don't know how to back-track."

"There are solutions to every problem," Alices said, quietly. "But I can't help you if I don't know what the problem is."

Evie snuffed out a laugh. "Believe it or not, the problem is that I'm pregnant."

"Ah," said Alice, knowing better than to say any more than that. She could see that Evie's eyes were red-rimmed, that she'd been crying.

"And rather than tell anyone, my best friend, say, or even my husband, who I really do adore, I ran off to London."

"Okay," Alice said.

"Which is dumb, because it's not like this problem is going away."

"And is it a problem?"

Evie blinked back tears and shrugged. "I don't know. No, I don't think so. But yes. I just... I never planned things this way, you know? I didn't want the traditional life. I have a job I love and... I'm just afraid that if I tell people then they'll expect me to have the baby and stay at home and give up everything that I love."

"I see." Alice leaned forward. "So you went to London so you could figure out what you want, without anyone else influencing your decision."

Evie's eyes sparked. "Exactly," she said. "That's exactly what I did. Maybe not my smartest move, but I felt like I had to. I couldn't deal with everyone else's expectations of what I would do or should do. Even Greg's."

"Your husband?"

Evie nodded.

Alice watched her carefully. "And do you want this child?"

"More than anything I think I've ever wanted before," Evie said quietly.

"Then that's your solution," said Alice. "If it's what you want, then you have to find a way to change your life to fit both your old desires and your new ones."

"Yes, you're right. I need to figure some stuff out." Evie frowned. "I don't suppose you...?"

Alice laughed. "I'm not really qualified, remember?" she said. "But if you ever need someone to talk to, then I'm happy to be a sounding board. Just give me a call. Viv has my number."

Speaking Viv's name aloud gave her a shiver in her stomach.

"I think I need to talk to your boss," Evie said, standing up. "Is he in?"

Alice nodded. "Through that door over there. And if you don't mind, I think I'll be making myself scarce for now."

"I might get a bit shouty," Evie said, grinning.

"I'll be sure to block my ears while I pack my stuff," Alice said, returning the grin.

She took her time, making sure that she packed everything into her purse. Not that she had much in the office, but she was fairly confident that she wouldn't be coming back here.

Then she took one last look at the place and turned to walk out.

Viv.

She needed to talk to Viv.

CHAPTER TWENTY SEVEN

As the evening got darker, the shadows in the living room grew and Viv didn't turn on the lights. She simply sat on the couch, arm around Max, trying to digest the day.

Evie pregnant. She understood, now that she'd been told, she got why Evie had done what she'd done. She was happy and excited for her, if a little anxious about what this change would mean for Evie's relationship with Greg, for Evie's career.

But it was Alice that occupied her mind far more.

The morning had been like an oasis in the desert, a little glimpse of what things could be like when the conditions were right.

But were those conditions right?

She thought so, but maybe she was wrong. Maybe her judgment was clouded. She'd let Alice into her life hard and fast, something she never did. The only other time she'd let someone get so close she'd ended up with her life shattered.

It was fully dark by the time the knock on the door came. She ignored it, but the door soon creaked open.

"I know you're there, Viv. I can see you through the living room window."

Max barked at the sound of Alice's voice. "I suppose you'd better come in then," Viv said.

There was the click of a switch and Viv blinked in the sudden light.

"Sitting in the dark and brooding wasn't at all what your life coach prescribed," Alice said, coming to sit on the other end of the couch.

Viv grunted. "I wasn't aware that I had a life coach anymore."

"I don't think you do," Alice said. "I left Evie yelling at Foster in the office. I think this plan might have been put to bed. Not that I don't think you should try again."

"No," Viv said. "I don't think so. I think I know myself better now, I think I can start to work toward fixing myself."

Alice shook her head. "You know this was never about fixing you, Viv. You're not broken. You're changed. There's nothing wrong with change, other than the fact that you find it difficult to deal with."

"Maybe," allowed Viv. She glanced over at Alice's profile. "Isn't it kind of late for you to be leaving work?"

Alice sighed. "My stupid car ran out of gas. I'm supposed to be the organized one, and you've got me running around in circles and forgetting to fill up the tank."

Viv smirked a little at this. "Glad to know that I have an influence on you just as much as you do on me."

"Of course you do," Alice said. "But things change, Viv. You have to come to accept that. It's important that you learn to deal with it. Change is a part of life."

Viv knew what was happening. She just didn't quite want to put words on it yet. Putting words on it would make it real and she really wasn't ready for reality. She wanted just a little more time in the oasis.

"This morning was amazing," she said. It felt like so long ago, a lifetime ago.

"I don't regret it," said Alice. "I don't ever want you to think that. I like you, Viv. I like you a lot."

"Not enough to think about being married to me," Viv said in a lame attempt to joke that hurt her even as she said it. Stupid, she thought to herself. As though she ever wanted to get married again. She didn't want anyone to think about her being married, but at the same time it hurt a little that Alice didn't. Maybe she was losing her mind.

"Not at first," Alice said. "But I changed. That's what makes you different, what makes you special. I think about every woman as marriage material immediately. But you, you had to grow on me."

"I'm a grumpy old lady," said Viv.

Alice's phone beeped with an incoming text and she took it out to check it, the small screen illuminating her face. Viv watched her, wanting to imprint the memory of her.

"Well, I'm finally out of a job," Alice said, putting the phone away. "I'm only surprised that it took this long."

"That asshole fired you by text?"

"Would you expect anything different?" Alice asked with a half-smile.

Viv grunted. "S'pose not. What are you going to do?"

"Change," Alice said. "I'll figure something out."

"You really should go into business for yourself," Viv said. "You've got a knack for this. Think about it."

Alice shook her head. "I don't think so. I don't think I've got the confidence to start my own business."

"You should. You've really helped me, Alice. I don't think I've ever thanked you for that."

Alice sighed. "You do know what's happening here, right?"

For a long time, Viv looked out of the front window, watching the shadows move in the front yard. "You're dumping me," she said, eventually. And when the world didn't stop turning at the words, she tried again. "We're breaking up. However you want to put it."

"It's not the right time, Viv. This wasn't the right way to go about things."

Evie's words lurked in the air. She knew next to nothing about Alice. "I know."

"And now I need to find a new job, and you need to use your new-found sense of self to build a life that's sustainable for you.

You need to let other people into your life, Viv. And stop being afraid of things changing. Change isn't always bad."

Which was easy to say but hard to believe since just at the moment things were changing in a way that seemed very bad to her indeed. Viv swallowed. "Right," she said in a small voice.

Alice shuffled closer. "You're an amazing woman, Viv. But Evie is right, you are in a vulnerable state and I shouldn't have taken advantage of that."

"You didn't."

"It's a fine line, and I'm not sure it wasn't crossed," said Alice. "But I do know that you need to find yourself, your new self, before you should become entangled with anyone else."

Which made sense, Viv thought. A car approached the house, lights sweeping over the lawn and momentarily blinding her.

"That's me," said Alice. "I need to go."

Every atom in Viv's body was crying out to stop her. Every physical part of her wanted to scream and shout and have a tantrum like a child and tell her not to leave.

Except for one little piece of her heart, that was yelling at her for stupidly, blindly trusting someone again. A little piece that shouldn't be able to outweigh everything else. A little piece whose voice should be drowned out by everything else.

But it was the little piece that won in the end.

"So this is goodbye."

"That's a little dramatic," Alice said. "I'm here. You have my number. If you need something, you can always call."

Viv nodded, knowing that she wouldn't call, knowing that she couldn't. She'd put herself out there once, she'd kissed Alice's soft lips in the library, taking that last step forward, bringing them so close together that she could feel Alice's breath on her cheeks.

She wasn't capable of opening up like that again.

She said nothing as Alice stood up.

"I'm sorry, Viv. Not sorry about what happened, but sorry that it needs to end like this. I do think it's necessary though. I think it's the right thing for both of us. These last few weeks have been intense. Perhaps it's natural that we got so close so fast."

Viv wished that she had the strength to stand up and kiss her one last time. But she didn't.

"Call me if you need me, Viv. I'm serious."

There was a long pause and then the sound of Alice's footsteps walking away, the front door creaking as it opened and snicking closed again.

Finally, Viv stood up. She walked to the window and watched as Alice walked down the steps and then toward the car at the end of the drive. She opened the door and the interior light flashed on for just a second.

A second that was long enough for Viv to see the profile of the woman in the driver's seat. Young, red-headed, tattoos snaking up her arms.

No, she thought, she knew nothing about Alice. Not really. She knew that she'd felt perfect in her arms, perfect when their lips touched. She didn't know who the woman in the car was. And she didn't know what could have been or should have been.

And she remembered what Cal had told her at the library. Sometimes, giving up is for realists.

She needed to be a realist about this. Just like Alice was being. Things would never have worked out, not when all Alice was looking for was a wife. Not when Viv couldn't handle change. Not when everything around her seemed to be falling to pieces again.

The car drove off and Viv watched the tail-lights disappear into the darkness.

It was better this way.

Alice hadn't always been honest. She had to remember that.

She'd learned her lesson about letting people get close. And she couldn't afford to forget what the price of letting someone in was. Not when Alice had worked so hard to help her recover.

CHAPTER TWENTY EIGHT

A lice sighed and seriously considered punching her keyboard, but settled for growling at it instead.

"Calm down there, Bingo," said Harrison, coming into the kitchen.

"Bingo?"

Harrison shrugged. "Seemed like a suitable dog name, you were growling. What's going on?"

"Job searching," Alice muttered.

"Uh-huh," said Harrison, pulling out a chair. "And the rest?"

"What rest?"

"You wouldn't speak in the car last night, you came in like a ghost and disappeared off to your room without a word. I'm not going to intrude if you don't want me to, but it seems pretty apparent that all is not well. I'm guessing you got fired?"

Alice nodded.

"And..." Harrison narrowed her eyes in thought. "And Viv," she said, finally.

"It's over."

It had been the only thing to do, the best thing to do. She should never have given into her urges like that. Okay, they were both adults, but Viv was in no position to get into a new relationship. And Alice was in no position to be involved in anything that wasn't a relationship.

"It's over?" Harrison said. "So it started?"

Alice blew out a big breath and started to talk as Harrison's eyes grew wider and wider.

"But... this is the woman you absolutely, definitely didn't think about marrying," Harrison said when Alice was done.

"I know," said Alice. "Something changed. I don't know what. She... I got used to her. I don't know. I can't explain it. It wasn't instant, it wasn't love at first sight, it was a sort of gradual realization."

"But it was wrong."

A spike went through her heart. "No," she said quietly. "It wasn't wrong. It should have been wrong, and I get that the circumstances weren't great, but for a second there it was perfect. For a minute I realized what I'd been waiting for, what it was all about."

Now Harrison sighed. "So why break it off?"

"Because continuing it would be wrong," Alice said. She'd thought about this, thought about it too much. "Viv needs to figure out who she is outside of a relationship. Losing her husband just about destroyed her, she'd based so much of who and what she was on the fact that she was married. Now she needs to learn to be herself before anything else."

"Oh, Al," Harrison said, reaching out and taking her hand. "That's sickeningly self-sacrificing, you know that, right?"

"What choice did I have?" Alice said. "Besides, I need to figure myself out too. I've got no job, you and I have no way of paying rent. I got my own stuff going on here."

Not to mention the fact that she needed time to re-evaluate. For as long as she could remember she'd wanted the perfect relationship, the perfect wife. And all of a sudden, she was prepared to choose something different, prepared to jump into bed with a woman who was unlikely to ever want to get married again.

Which shouldn't be a big deal, wasn't a big deal, not really. Except it made Alice wonder what else she'd been wrong about, in what other ways she thought she knew herself but didn't.

"We're going to be just fine," Harrison was saying. "I've got an interview this afternoon. As for you, you'll find something, you always do." She hesitated before adding: "What about this life coaching thing?"

"What about it?" Alice asked absently, scrolling through another job site.

"Well, you enjoyed it, didn't you?"

"Sure." Another pang of pain. Would she enjoy it without Viv there though?

"And you seemed to be pretty good at it."

"What's your point?"

Harrison shrugged. "It doesn't really require any qualifications, I'm just saying that you could go into business for yourself if this is what you want. It wouldn't be too complicated."

"Seriously?" Alice said, looking up. "Not complicated? Where would I find clients? What about strategies and marketing?"

"What about any other excuse you can think of?" countered Harrison.

Another big breath. "Sorry. I'm being defensive. Viv told me the same thing."

"Then maybe you should think about it. Maybe it wouldn't be as difficult as you think," Harrison said. She squeezed Alice's hand. "You're good at helping people, Al. And maybe this is what you need, a real calling in life, something to take your mind off the fact that you're not walking down the aisle just yet."

Alice kept her attention on the screen. "I'll think about it," she said, with no intention at all of sparing it another moment's thought. She had bills to pay. She needed to be realistic here.

SHE HAD JUST stepped out of the shower when she heard the phone ringing. She couldn't help it. Her heart sped up, her fingers fumbled for a towel. Maybe it was Viv, maybe...

Maybe what?

Nothing had changed. Her decision was as right as it had been the night before. She picked up the phone anyway, heart in her throat.

"Alice?"

"Cal? Is that you?"

"Your favorite librarian," Cal laughed. "Although, not for much longer, I'm afraid."

"Yes, I heard," Alice said, perching on the edge of her bed. "I'm sorry, Cal. I know you worked hard to keep the place open."

"Not all stories have happy endings," said Cal. "Something that I seem to be reminding people a lot these days."

"No," Alice agreed. "But some stories deserve a better ending than others, don't you think?"

Cal chuckled. "Things happen for the best, in my opinion. This seems like a blow, but maybe it's just the universe preparing me for something new."

Alice closed her eyes and wished she could believe anything as optimistic as that. It had scared her a little, in truth, just how much she'd wanted Viv to be on the other end of the line.

"You sound a little down, is everything okay?" Cal asked.

"It's fine."

"Oh, well good. I just wanted to touch base with you," said Cal, sounding not at all put out that Alice had snapped. "You and Viv helped a lot with the fundraiser, and we're not quite dead yet. We're having a book sale a week from Saturday. I know that doesn't sound immensely exciting, but there'll be drinks after and some of us will stick around re-living old times and cleaning the place out. I'd like to invite the two of you."

Alice cleared her throat. "Oh, uh, that's very kind of you."

"You'll be there, won't you?"

Cal sounded almost pleading and Alice didn't have the heart to say no. "Of course I will," she said. "I can't speak for Viv though. I'm afraid we're..." Ouch. The pain was almost tangible. She cleared her throat again. "We're..." She couldn't finish the sentence. She really didn't know how to.

"Oh," said Cal. "Oh, well, I'll give her a call." She paused. "Are you really alright, Alice?"

"Absolutely fine."

"If you need someone to talk to..."

"I'm fine," Alice said again. "But thank you."

"Of course," said Cal.

They said their goodbyes and hung up and Alice just for a moment thought about calling Viv.

She wanted to talk to her, wanted to hear her grumpy hello, wanted to have coffee and discuss how they'd spend their day. It was just the time when she'd be arriving at the front door, just the time when Viv would be grumbling about interfering life coaches and best friends.

"It's all for the best," she told herself. Maybe Cal was right. Maybe she had to do this, go through this, so that she could find something better at the end of it.

Except her gut was telling her that there was nothing better than Viv. Whatever her ideals had been, whatever she'd thought she wanted, the sense of completion she'd felt in Viv's arms couldn't have been for nothing.

It had to be for nothing.

Neither one of them were in a position to do anything about anything. End of story.

"You know, you might have been wrong."

Alice turned to see Harrison leaning on the doorframe. "Wrong?"

"You told Viv that she was afraid of change."

"She is," Alice said.

"And yet she was the one that was willing to let you into her life, into her bed, and you're the one running away from it," Harrison said. "You're the one that's looking for the same old assistant jobs instead of thinking about something new."

"Harrison..."

"It's just a thought," Harrison said. "That's all. Now I've used up my very last clean and ironed shirt and I've got that interview this afternoon, so I've come to raid your closet."

"Have you indeed?"

"Well, ordinarily, you wouldn't be here to see me doing it," Harrison said, with a grin. "So, think of it this way, at least you're getting informed this time."

Alice sighed and stood up to open her closet as Harrison started to sort through her shirts.

Afraid of change. As if.

CHAPTER
TWENTY NINE

Viv grunted and turned the volume up. If she made the TV loud enough then she couldn't hear the kids playing outside.

It was taking every shred of patience she had not to open the window and yell at them. She gritted her teeth and glared at the TV.

Max whined.

"What?"

He whined again, tilting his head to one side and watching her.

"Fuck." Her fifth fuck of the day. "Come on then."

She unraveled herself from the blankets on the couch and pulled a hoodie on before clipping Max's leash to his collar.

"Make this fast though, there's a John Wayne Gacy show coming on in a half hour," she grumbled, as she led him out of the house.

"Morning, Viv," Mr. Webber called from his porch.

She bared her teeth at him in a way that, as far as she could tell, he assumed made up a smile, and then stalked down the road with Max.

"Do you have to be so picky about which tree you use?" she asked him, as they rounded the corner of the street. "Come on, this one looks good, let's go Max."

Max whined again, then obediently peed up against the tree.

"Right. Good. See? At least you're not afraid of change. A different damn tree every time. Home again, Max. Come on, good boy."

She turned around and they went back the way they came.

There were no feelings there.

It was the same problem she'd had after Bill had left.

People kept asking her how she felt, they kept bringing casseroles and bottles of wine so she could drown her sorrows. They kept expecting her to talk about things.

But there was nothing to talk about.

In her brain she knew what had happened, she was well aware of the fact that Alice wasn't coming back and that they wouldn't be together and there'd be no more mornings or bungee jumps or anything else.

But it was like everything else had switched off. She was... blank. She felt blank. Tired, maybe, that was the best she could come up with. Empty perhaps. But explaining her feelings? How was she supposed to do that when everything was switched off?

Besides, what was the point? Alice had made her decision. And Alice was probably right anyway. She generally was about most things.

She was afraid of change. She hated change. The last time her life had changed and almost stopped. Like a train getting derailed. So obviously she was wary this time around. Evie was right too, in her way. She knew nothing about Alice.

Nothing except that her hair smelled of citrus and her skin felt like silk and her mouth tasted of toothpaste and coffee and cinnamon.

She stopped in the middle of the sidewalk.

For a moment she thought she might be sick.

Which was the problem with feeling. Not feeling was fine, it was numb and comforting. Suddenly start to feel something and all of a sudden you felt like you might lose your breakfast onto the tarmac.

"Come on, Max," she said, tugging at the leash.

As she approached the house, the children scattered from where they'd been playing close to the property line, making for the safety of the porch.

"Hey, Viv," Webber shouted.

Viv groaned. She couldn't handle a conversation, not right now. "What?"

"There's someone in there," he said. "A woman, I know you know her though, so I didn't think—"

Viv didn't hear the rest of what he thought because she was too busy tripping up the steps and pushing through the door and letting Max's leash go and turning into the living room... to see Evie sitting on the couch.

"It's you," she said, accusingly.

"It is, indeed, me. I see that your eyesight hasn't deteriorated over the last few days."

"What are you doing here?"

Evie rolled her eyes. "You get dumped, you tell me all about it, then you don't answer my calls for three days and leave me on read. What do you think I'm doing here, Viv?"

"You didn't have to come." Viv kicked off her sneakers and curled back up in the corner of the couch she liked so much.

"Yes, Viv, yes I did." Evie reclined back into the couch herself, grabbing the remote. "So, what are we watching? Jack the Ripper? Ted Bundy?"

"John Wayne Gacy," Viv mumbled as Evie flicked the TV on.

For half an episode, they sat together, eyes glued to the screen, not moving or speaking. Until Evie finally dimmed the volume as the ads came on.

"Are we doing this again, Viv?" she asked.

"Doing what?"

"This. Disappearing away from the world again."

Viv bit her lip but didn't answer.

"You can't do this, Viv. Not again. You were improving, becoming more and more like your old self. You can't regress like this."

"My old self?" The words sent a cold shiver down her spine. "My old self? That's all you want back, isn't it? You just want things to go back to the way they were before like nothing happened, like Bill never left, like my life never turned upside down."

"No, no, Viv, don't—"

"That's why you paid all that money for a life coach. Just to get back some old version of me that you liked. Maybe you don't like the new version so much, huh? Maybe that's why you didn't tell me about the baby. Maybe that's why you just disappeared off to London."

Evie moved, turning. "Viv—"

"What the hell kind of best friend are you supposed to be? Huh?"

Evie stood up. "Seriously? You're going to come after me now? After everything I did? I didn't try to get the old you back, I tried to get any version of you that I could back. I don't know how the hell my confident, sparky, sarcastic best friend turned into the kind of old lady that scares kids, but I do know that that isn't you."

"How? How do you know that? You're not even here."

"Wanna know why I didn't tell you about the baby?" Evie said, hands on hips. "Because just for once, I thought I'd be you. I thought that I'd shut everyone out and deal with my own things in my own time. And guess what? It didn't work."

"Bullshit."

"It didn't work because I can't make decisions like this alone. And neither can you. You keep shutting people out, Viv, and you're going to become a recluse. You're going to have no one, no one will care for you, no one will call for you, no one will think of you. Is that really what you want?"

"Why would you care?"

"Because, believe it or not Vivien Curtis, you are my best damn friend in the world and I'm fucked if I'm going to let you die alone in your bed so that cats eat your face off."

Viv blinked. Evie rarely cursed. She was the one with a mouth like a sailor. Not Evie.

Evie took a deep, shuddering breath. "I'm sorry if me trying to help you was such an imposition. I'm sorry that I stumbled into your life. And I'm sorry that you're not happy, Viv. But I'm sick and tired of watching you settle for unhappiness, like you don't want anything else, like you're not willing to fight for anything else."

"I'm not unhappy," Viv said.

"Really? Sitting here all alone with Max watching creepy serial killers and yelling at the kids on your lawn? That's what makes you happy?"

Viv stuck out her lip. "Sure, yeah, why not?"

Evie closed her eyes for a second, then opened them again. "Because there's a whole world out there, Viv. A whole shining, beautiful world with new people and hearts and experiences and places, just waiting to be discovered, just waiting for you to take a step outside of yourself and open your eyes. But you don't seem to want to do that, you seem to be perfectly happy being blind."

Viv swallowed and said nothing.

"Fine," said Evie, rolling her eyes once more. "Fine. I won't interfere anymore. If this is you being happy, then go ahead and wallow in your happiness. I'm done here."

She grabbed her jacket from the armchair and slung her bag over her shoulder.

Viv closed her eyes so that she didn't have to watch.

But she heard the door slam, heard Evie's footsteps echo down the drive. Then she heard silence.

For a heartbeat she waited, thinking that maybe Evie would come back. Only when she didn't did she reach for the remote.

She turned the sound back up.

Screw Evie and her interfering. Screw what anyone else thought. She could be happy like this.

Max whined again and she patted the couch until he jumped up beside her.

"We're happy, right Max?"

He settled down with his head on her lap and she turned her

attention to the TV.

CHAPTER THIRTY

Alice pushed open the office door and then paused. Something was wrong.

The magazines were still splayed out on the table. The walls were still white and sterile.

But there was no one sitting behind the reception desk.

She frowned. It wasn't like she wanted to be here. Returning to the scene of the crime didn't exactly make her feel better.

She'd had a lot of time to think about the mistakes she'd made working for Foster Davison, and a lot of time to consider how she should have done things differently. Refusing to pose as a life coach was the obvious thing. She shouldn't have done it and would now be more careful about what she agreed to.

It was more than that though.

She should never have worked for Davison in the first place. He was an asshole, as Harrison so nicely put it. He barked orders and had no morals, and she couldn't think of anyone she'd more like to slap.

Especially since she was yet to see any kind of pay check.

Which explained why she was walking into the strangely deserted offices of Foster Davison, Life Coach.

"Hello?"

Her voice echoed around the empty reception area.

Nothing. Not a sound.

For God's sake.

Alice steeled herself and then marched down the corridor. She deserved to be paid and she wasn't going to let Davison cheat her out of what she was owed. Especially since she'd done so much for him.

She yanked at the door to what had once been her office, eyes fixed on Foster's closed office door that lay behind her ex-desk. She was half-way across the carpet before she realized someone was rifling through filing cabinets.

"Excuse me?"

"Who— ow!" The woman stood up too fast and knocked her head on the edge of an open drawer. She winced and turned so that Alice could see that it was the cool, blonde receptionist. "Ah."

"I'm looking for Foster Davison," Alice said, politely.

"You and about half the town," said the receptionist, collapsing in the desk chair and rubbing at her head. "Sorry, can you see? Is it bleeding?"

Alice stepped in closer and peered at the woman's head. "Nope," she said. "No blood, but it sounded like a hard bang. You're going to have a headache in a little while."

"Just what I need," grimaced the receptionist. She sighed and looked up at Alice. "It's Alice, right?"

Alice nodded.

"I'm Jolene. I don't think we ever really got properly introduced. You weren't in the office much, what with Foster being sick and all."

Alice was about to reply with a little added small talk when Jolene's words finally sank in. "What do you mean, half the town is looking for him?"

The receptionist raised her eyebrows. "You mean you haven't heard?"

"Heard what?"

Jolene scowled. "How don't you know? I mean it was pretty obvious yesterday when... Come to think of it, I didn't see you yesterday. Or the day before either."

Alice decided there was no harm in telling the truth. "I, um, got fired. Last week."

"Huh, lucky you," Jolene said.

"Lucky? I wouldn't exactly say that."

"Well, at least you don't need to deal with the fallout of all this," said Jolene, waving her hands around the office like it would explain something.

Alice took a seat on the edge of the desk. Clearly, Foster wasn't here. "All what, exactly?" she asked. "What's going on?"

"Foster's left. Disappeared. Emptied out the company accounts and gone AWOL."

Alice's stomach flipped over. "I guess that explains why I didn't get paid."

"You neither?" asked Jolene, finally removing her hand from her head. "He's screwed everyone over, and I've no idea why."

"Well, the company wasn't exactly doing well," Alice said. "I've seen the books and the numbers."

"That's no one's fault but Foster's," said Jolene. "I get a half dozen calls a day from new clients. But he only takes on the ones he thinks are easy fixes. Or maybe the ones with cute butts or nice eyes or something, I don't know."

"He didn't want his clients?"

Jolene sighed. "I think he only wanted the big name clients. You know, the ones who he could put on his website, the ones that made him look like he was a someone. Which doesn't make sense, because there are plenty of people out there who wanted his services and could pay for them."

It was Alice's turn to sigh. Without a pay check she could just about cover this month's rent and groceries. After that though, she'd be dead broke. She'd better find another job and find it fast. "He'll be in Mexico by now," she said.

"Or Costa Rica," agreed Jolene. "Meanwhile, I'm left holding the bag. I guess I should just walk out, but then my boyfriend said that there was all kinds of personal information in files here and that probably I should tell the police what had happened and, well, to be honest, I thought I'd have a look around to see if there was anything of value."

Alice raised one eyebrow.

"What? I didn't get paid either," Jolene pouted.

"Well, I guess there's no chance of collecting now," said Alice, standing up again. "I'll get out of your hair. Good luck with all this."

Jolene shrugged. "I'm about to leave it all to the accountants and the police," she said. "I'll lock up on my way out."

"I guess it was nice finally meeting you." She turned to leave.

"Hey, hold on a second," Jolene said. "You should take some of this stuff."

"Like what?" Alice said. "I don't have space for another desk chair at home, besides, it would seem like stealing."

"That's not what I'm talking about," Jolene said. She was tapping at the computer now, her other hand scrabbling in the desk drawer and coming out with a flash drive. "Give me a second."

"Then what are you talking about?"

"You were his assistant, right?" Jolene said, still busy at the computer.

"Yes, but not in the way you might be thinking," Alice started, preparing herself to make her explanations all over again.

"Then you should take this," said Jolene, yanking out the flash drive and handing it over.

"What is it?" Alice asked.

"Everything. At least as far as I can tell. It's Foster's entire client list, including those that called to inquire and he never followed up on. All the templates he used for contracts and the like. All his method sheets. It's everything that was in his personal file on the network."

Alice looked at the drive. "I don't know..."

"Oh, just take it. You can set up shop yourself with this info. You might as well. You could be the next Foster Davison. Well, a more attractive and ethical version, I hope."

"Oh, I don't want to go into life coaching," Alice said quickly.

"Take it anyway," Jolene advised. "You might change your mind. Besides, you're not likely to get anything else out of this place, so you might as well take something."

And Alice was too tired to argue. She pocketed the flash drive and thanked Jolene, wishing her luck again before leaving the office.

The drive weighed down her pocket as she walked.

Everything weighed her down just at the minute.

It's only been a week, she told herself, as she left Foster Davison's building for the last time.

A week, and she still startled every time the phone rang. She still smiled when she woke up, thinking of Viv's face, until she remembered that she wouldn't be seeing her.

Maybe she should do something.

Maybe life coaching wasn't so bad.

Maybe she could do this.

It would give her something to take her mind off everything else, at least.

But then, she wasn't sure she could forget the feel of Viv's lips on hers. She could definitely never forget the image of Viv leaning back against the bookshelf, hair messed up, legs stretching down to high heels, jacket half-buttoned and lips swollen.

A jolt went through her at the very memory.

Then she started to vibrate and it took a second to realize that her phone was ringing in her jacket pocket.

"Al?" Harrison's voice bounced over the line. "You'll never guess what. I got it!"

"Got what?" Alice asked.

"The job! I got the job, we're not going to be bankrupt. Pressure's off, baby. We're back in the game."

Alice forced herself to smile. "Congratulations," she said.

But she couldn't make herself feel happy. She hadn't felt happy for ages. She hadn't even smiled properly.

Not since she'd left Viv's house for the last time.

CHAPTER THIRTY ONE

V iv took a deep breath and pressed the icon on her phone to call Evie.

It was time to apologize, she wasn't about to let her best friend go. She hated it when Evie was mad at her. And she'd had time to think about what Evie had said. She wasn't entirely wrong. Something needed to change. Whatever else Viv was, she wasn't happy, and it was time to admit that.

But there was no answer, so she lay back on the bed and groaned. "What if she's ignoring me, Max?"

Max woofed in response and her phone buzzed. A text. Evie.

Viv swallowed back a sigh of relief. She knew Evie wouldn't ditch her. They'd always had their fights, but she truly felt bad about the day before. And she knew it was up to her to start the groveling, Evie deserved it.

On way to airport. Running late. Will call later.

Viv read the text and closed the app.

Nope.

No way.

Evie wasn't going to leave the country like this. Not on her watch.

"You'll be okay for a while here, Max, right?"

She was already pulling on sneakers, already grabbing her

keys. She lived way closer to the airport than Evie did, there was a fair chance she was going to make it in more than enough time to at least hug Evie goodbye.

With that thought, she ran out of the door and jumped into her SUV.

IT WAS ONLY once she'd skidded into a short-term parking space that Viv really considered what she was doing. What were the chances of her running into Evie in the middle of an airport? But she was here now, she'd just have to trust to fate.

The morning was warm and sunny and she had to shield her eyes as she looked up and down the sidewalk outside the doors to the departure lounge. She was about to give up hope, or about to go inside and grab a coffee at least, when she saw the back of a familiar looking head.

"Greg?"

Greg turned and frowned. "Viv? What are you doing here?"

She could feel herself blush. "Um, waiting for Evie."

"Ah, making up before she flies off, right?"

"You know that we fought?"

Greg grinned. "I know everything, Viv. At least now I do anyway. And if I were you, I wouldn't worry too much. It was a little fight, you both said things you now regret, I'm sure it's going to be fine."

"Really?" Viv said, somewhat suspiciously. Then she noticed the luggage cart by Greg's side. "Wait, are these yours?"

Greg looked down absently and nodded, before going back to scanning the oncoming traffic, looking for Evie.

"You're going too?" It made sense that Evie was going back to London. She'd have loose ends to tie up, if nothing else. But Greg? Greg who was always too busy with his own business, his own career, to make it to dinner or to drinks?

Now he turned and looked at her properly. "Yes," he said. "I'm going."

"But... but why?"

Greg looked at the traffic one more time, then gestured toward a bench. "How about we sit down?"

Viv followed him. The metal of the bench was cool against her legs.

"I know you and I haven't always gotten along as well as we should. I know that you're important to Evie, and I should have made more of an effort," he said, when they were seated.

Viv shrugged. She hadn't exactly given things that much thought. Greg was Greg, she wasn't the one married to him.

"But Evie is the most important thing in my life, bar none. I might sometimes forget that. I might sometimes wish for different circumstances. But I never, ever wish for a different person. So yes, I'm going with her to London so she can finish out her contract there."

"You're taking, what, four months off to go live in London?" Viv asked, truly surprised.

"I'm taking four months off to go and support my pregnant wife in doing what she loves," Greg amended. "Because she needs me there and so that's where I'll be. It's that simple."

"That's... quite the sacrifice," Viv said, not really knowing what else to say.

"What about you?" Greg asked. "Come to your senses yet?"

"What's that supposed to mean?"

He looked at the traffic, then looked back. "It means that it literally took my wife running away from me to make me realize that I haven't always made the right decisions when it came to her. And when I looked at myself, truly looked, and realized what she means to me, then making the right decision was actually pretty easy."

"I don't see the connection."

"I know about you and Alice," he said.

"Still not seeing it, Greg."

He sighed. "I don't know what everyone else has been telling you, Viv. And I can only tell you what I know to be true for me. But when something matters, really matters, then everything else stops mattering for a little while, do you see what I mean?"

Viv did, but didn't want to admit it. Where did this guy get off telling her what to do anyway?

"Okay, it's none of my business," Greg said. "So I'll tell you something else instead."

"Like what?"

He leaned back on the bench, one hand still on the luggage trolley. "Evie makes my world a lighter place. A better place. Don't get me wrong, I can live without her, but I would never want to. She makes getting up every morning just a little bit easier. And I think that's all anyone can ask of another person, to share the load, to help carry the weight of life."

For a moment Viv thought about Alice, thought about waking up next to her, thought about how much more she had smiled with Alice around.

"There will always be problems, there'll always be sacrifices and those that judge you. There will always be excuses for why something couldn't or shouldn't happen," Greg said, eyes on the incoming cars.

"Tell me about it," Viv muttered.

"But then, at the end of the day, you just have to decide what you want and then you have to go get it."

"You make that sound like a trip to the store to grab ice cream."

Greg grinned and for a second Viv saw what Evie saw in him. "It's not much different, I guess. You know what you want, so you make the effort to go get it. And yes, sometimes the store is out of ice cream, or sometimes you don't quite get the kind you thought you wanted, but that's all part of the fun."

Viv tilted her head to one side. "To be clear, you're equating the possible love of my life to ice cream?"

Another grin. "You said it, not me. The possible love of your life. So, let me ask you this, Viv. If Alice is the love of your life, what kind of person would you be to let her just walk away?"

"She doesn't want to be with me, Greg. She's the one making excuses."

"You're the one listening to them," he said. "I get that you've been beaten down, Viv. I get why you might not want to take a risk. But life is a risk. All of it. Crossing the street is a risk. Coming here today to try and find Evie was a risk. If there's something you want, or someone, you have to make an effort, you have to break out of your shell and show that person what they really mean to you."

He put a hand on her shoulder.

"Otherwise, what's the point? It would be like going through life without sunshine. Possible, but very, very dreary." He smiled at her. "I guess what I'm saying is, I don't know you all that well. But I know more about you than you think. And I don't buy what everyone's saying about you not liking change, not wanting to move on. I think you're just waiting for the right opportunity to change for, you're waiting until the risk is really worth the reward."

"I am?"

He nodded. "And if Alice made you smile half as much as Evie makes me smile, well, then I'm telling you that the risk is really, really worth it."

She was about to speak, but he was standing up, waving, and she turned to see Evie dragging suitcases out of a cab.

"Viv, what are you doing here?" Evie screeched.

"Apologizing."

Evie practically threw herself into Viv's arms. "No apology necessary, we were both cranky idiots. And I'm running so late that if I'm not careful we'll be swimming to London. I love you, I'll call you when we get there, and we'll be home soon, I promise."

She smacked a kiss on both of Viv's cheeks and let her go, grabbing up suitcases as Greg hurried her along.

"Safe trip," Viv said, unable to stop herself smiling as Greg picked up both of Evie's suitcases and threw them onto the trolley.

"Remember what I said," Greg shouted.

Evie turned around. "You still sad?"

"A little."

"Then go find Alice."

"I thought you were totally against the idea and thought she took advantage of my vulnerable state," Viv said in surprise.

"I can be wrong," Evie grinned. "Look at me now, going to London with the husband that I thought would never stop working. We all make mistakes, Viv. The only thing we can do is try and fix them."

"Alice wasn't a mistake," Viv said without really thinking about the words.

Evie grinned as Greg started to pull her away. "Then go get the girl!"

CHAPTER
THIRTY TWO

"**A**lmost ready?" Harrison said, sticking her head around the door.

"Like, two minutes," said Alice, pinning her hair back. She eyed her roommate. "Feeling good?"

"Feeling relieved," said Harrison. "And can't wait to have a celebratory drink. I know that you took that job for me, Al. I know that you stuck with it for me, at least at first. And I don't want you to think that I don't appreciate it."

"Well, you might be returning the favor more quickly than you'd like," Alice said, standing up from her dressing table.

"Which I will be glad to do," said Harrison. "This job is a good one, I can feel it in my bones. I loved the interview, I loved the office, I can't wait to get started."

Alice couldn't help but smile at her enthusiasm. She didn't particularly feel like going out, she felt more like sitting in bed and watching Netflix. But Harrison deserved a little fun.

"Hey, where's your thing?" asked Harrison, pointing at the wall.

"What thing?"

"The thing, that board you had, the one with the wedding dresses and stuff on it."

"My mood board?" Alice asked. She shrugged. "I got rid of it."

Harrison shook her head. "Oh, girl. We got some stuff to talk about. Come on. Let's get a drink in front of you and some sense inside you. Get moving."

Obedient as ever, Alice followed her out of the room.

THE BAR WAS a quiet one, not at all the bright, noisy, pick-up joint that Alice had imagined Harrison would choose. They sat in a little booth at the back and Alice chose a fruity cocktail at Harrison's insistence.

"Money's coming in again, you should get what pleases you. In fact, that should be a general rule in life from now on."

"Getting what pleases me?" Alice asked. "That just sounds like you're trying to turn me into a thief."

Harrison shook her head, ordered drinks, then settled into the booth. "Alright, real talk time. What's up with the mood board?"

"Do you think I'm an idiot?"

"Huh? That's a pretty broad question. I'm going to need you to be more specific," Harrison grinned.

"All the wedding stuff and the getting married and all that. I feel like maybe I've been a romantic about it, a child about it, I don't know. I think it's time that I grow up a little, and getting rid of the mood board was part of that."

Harrison sighed. "I don't think there's anything wrong with wanting to fall in love," she said. "I don't think there's anything wrong with wanting a wife or wanting to be one. But I also don't think that you truly know what you want."

Part of Alice wanted to dispute this, and Harrison must have seen it on her face.

"Al, you're only twenty five. You come here and you take assistant jobs and it looks like you're just waiting around to find Ms. Right. But truthfully, I kind of think that you were waiting to find yourself."

"Past tense?"

"Well, didn't you find it?"

Alice frowned and a drink appeared in front of her.

"Al, tell me for real right now, this life coaching thing. It's your thing, right? It's what you're good at, it's something that gives you pleasure, a job you can wake up every morning and look forward to doing?"

She took a long drink of the tart cocktail and blinked away a tear from the sting of orange juice. "Harrison..."

"No, be honest, just between the two of us."

"Um, maybe."

"Maybe? Which is why you've been staring at Foster Davison's client list for the last two days. Make any calls yet?"

"A couple."

"And?"

Alice bit her lip. "And there's a couple of people who want help. I told them I'm not qualified. I told them I'm inexperienced. They seemed okay with it, happy to have me learn on the job as long as I offer a discounted price."

"Which is how you get experience, Al, that's fine."

"And I looked into some classes. Psych classes at the community college. I could start next semester."

"You've already started planning this, Al. So what's the problem?"

She had. She hadn't been able to help herself. Her natural tendency to want to organize had stepped in and before she knew it she was making a plan for just how this could work. She knew, deep down, that Harrison was right, that Viv had been right. She liked helping people, she liked organizing things, this job was a match made in heaven.

"I feel like I'm, I don't know, betraying myself? Does that make sense?"

Harrison laughed long and loud before knocking back a solid quarter of her vodka and tonic. "Listen here, kiddo, people change and there's nothing wrong with that. Wanting more out of life isn't a bad thing. Making a plan for yourself, a career, isn't a bad thing. Deciding what you want isn't a bad thing. Do you see a running theme here?"

"But..."

"But nothing, Al. Maybe you were a romantic, maybe you still are. But I'm a firm believer in making yourself happy so you can make someone else happy. Besides, you're not giving up on the idea of getting married and living happily ever after, are you?"

"No..." Alice said even though she wasn't so sure.

"Then what's the problem? You're allowed to choose more than one thing that makes you happy, you know?"

"I guess," said Alice.

Harrison held up her glass. "So, I guess we're celebrating two new jobs then, aren't we? Me finally being employed again, and you setting up your own business, which is quite impressive."

Alice clinked her glass against Harrison's and smiled. "Yeah, it is a little, isn't it?"

"More than a little," Harrison said, drinking. "But we're not done here yet, my girl. I'm glad about the coaching business, I'll help you any way you need, just ask. But there's one more thing."

"What's that?" The cocktail really was quite good. She could feel herself relaxing for what felt like the first time in weeks.

"Viv."

Even the name made Alice's toes curl up, made a shiver go down her back. She had to swallow to get enough moisture in her mouth to speak properly. "What about her?"

"That's my question," Harrison said. "You had feelings for her, didn't you?"

Alice nodded. "I don't know how or why. I think she was the first woman I met that I didn't imagine walking down the aisle with."

A look of pity crossed Harrison's face. "And there's no hope now?"

"I can't," Alice said. "Not that I don't want to, I truly do. I'm not the type to sit around feeling sorry for myself, but I can admit that my life is a little darker, a little less good without Viv in it. I did the right thing though, I know that. She's vulnerable and I can't take advantage of that."

"She's an adult, you could let her make her own decisions," said Harrison.

"The moment has passed. She needs to decide what she wants in her life, she needs to figure herself out properly."

Harrison rolled her eyes. "You're being a martyr. How do you know she's not just sitting around feeling sorry for herself about you?"

"I don't."

"Jesus, Al. If you're meant for each other, then why does it matter how you met or anything else?"

"She was—"

"In a vulnerable state, yes, I know. But she's also an adult, you helped her start to find herself again, and you don't get to make all the rules in the world, Al. If you make her happy and she makes you happy then who the hell cares?"

Alice spun her cocktail glass between her hands, her fingers getting cold. "Maybe you're right," she said, wanting Harrison to be right, but fearing that she wasn't. Fearing that once she'd left, Viv had realized what a bad idea it was for the two of them to be together and had moved on.

"So what are you going to do about it?"

"Nothing," she said, firmly. "I'm going to do absolutely nothing about it. It is what it is and, like you said, if it's meant to be then something will happen, right?"

"Yeah, not what I meant."

"I can't push this, Harrison. Not after I gave in and slept with her and then ended things. It wouldn't be right for me to show up again demanding that she be with me. I'd be tipping her world over again, and that's the last thing she needs."

Harrison's eyes narrowed. "But you're going to see her at this library thing, right?"

"The book sale? Maybe," Alice said, knowing that she was hoping for exactly that but not knowing whether or not Viv would go without her.

"Uh-huh. Want to borrow my red dress again?"

Alice felt a buzz in her chest, a trickle of warmth, just a touch of hope. "It's not that kind of party."

"Doesn't hurt to dress the part," Harrison said airily. "Now, how about another of those cocktails? I feel like we should be celebrating a whole lot more than just me getting a job."

CHAPTER THIRTY THREE

V iv placed the carton of books down on the table. "So, what do you think?" she asked.

"What do I think about what?" said Cal, depositing her own book carton.

"About... everything."

Cal leaned against the edge of the table, crossing her arms. "I think you've had an awful lot of advice from an awful lot of people."

Viv nodded.

"And I think that we've worked our butts off here and that it's time for a coffee."

Viv followed her through to the library's small back room and sat down on a couch as Cal poured coffees for them both. "So, you don't have any advice then?"

"Don't you have enough of that?" asked Cal, handing over the mug. "Here's a thing: what do you want?"

"I want Alice back in my life."

"Are you sure?"

"Certain. I have feelings, Cal, I can't ignore them. I know that I barely know the woman, but I want a chance to discover her, a chance to find out what we could have."

"Okay. And what if she turns you down?"

"Then I'll have to take that and move on with my life," Viv said. "I'm not the delicate little flower that everyone seems to think I am. Or at least, I'm not anymore. I need to give this a try. One last shot. I need to find out for sure, because if I keep going like this I'm going to end up bitter and full of regret."

"Mmm, the last thing the world needs is you any more bitter."

"Ha ha, very funny. Look, I get it, I get all the objections. I get why Alice walked away, I really do. But I need to put myself first here, I need to make decisions for me, and I want to give this another shot."

"How are you planning on persuading Alice to give things another shot?" asked Cal, blowing gently across the surface of her coffee.

"By communicating openly and properly," said Viv as though she was reciting a lesson.

"Glad I've taught you something," laughed Cal. "But I was talking more about the specifics."

Viv sipped at her own mug. "She thinks that I'm afraid of change, and nothing could be further from the truth right now. Everyone kept telling me to get back to my old self, but that was bullshit. I need to find a new self, just like Alice said."

"Are you a new self?"

"I'm working on it," Viv said.

She'd thought about this a lot. Thought about sitting on her couch and watching TV until she and Max were practically FBI profilers thanks to their knowledge of serial killers and true crime.

She'd thought about what she'd wanted life to be, how Bill had changed her, how she'd allowed herself to be changed.

And she'd thought more about Alice than she'd ever thought about anyone before in her life.

"Here's the thing," she said now to Cal. "With Bill I had the picture perfect life. A husband, a house in the suburbs, a career, a dog. When he left, that picture got shattered. I think my problem was that I didn't know what to replace it with. I didn't have another model for how life could or should be. So I gave up trying."

"And now you know what you want life to be?"

"I'm getting there," Viv said.

"You know how you want life to be with or without Alice in it?"

"I'm not going back to that old self," Viv said. "And that includes the self that sits around in front of the Discovery Channel all day."

"That seems like a fairly healthy mindset to me, I suppose." Cal took a drink from her coffee and grimaced. "You know, the coffee in here has always been terrible. It's the one thing that I won't miss at all."

"What are you going to do?" asked Viv.

Cal shrugged. "I've been focused on closing this place down. But I'll look for another job. Luckily, Lea's successful enough for both of us. I might have to be a kept woman for a while."

It was Viv's turn to grimace. "Being a kept woman is over-rated."

Cal laughed. "Do you have a plan here?" she asked. "Like, I don't know, sending a thousand red roses? Singing outside her balcony?"

"I don't think Alice has a balcony," Viv said. "I've never been to her place." She was struck by a momentary doubt, which she recognized and dismissed. "I'm not pretending to know everything about her, I'm asking for a chance to get to know more about her."

"Impressive attitude," Cal said.

"It's something Alice taught me," admitted Viv. "I need to recognize my feelings and decide whether they're appropriate to the situation or not."

"Huh, she really is pretty good at this life coaching thing."

"She is," affirmed Viv. "And as for grand gestures, I don't know. That's why I'm asking your advice. I watch more bloody murders than romantic comedies. What are the kids doing nowadays?"

"Um, making silly TikTok videos, I think."

"What's a TikTok?" Viv asked.

Cal shook her head. "Maybe a grand gesture isn't what you need," she said. "Maybe you need something a little more subtle."

"Like what?"

"Well, I do have one small idea." Cal beckoned and Viv leaned in close, a grin spreading over her face as Cal whispered in her ear.

"HEY, CAN I play with your dog?"

The little face that was looking up at her was covered in something that Viv hoped was chocolate, the cheeks were red and the child was almost breathless.

"Maddie, leave Viv alone," Mr. Webber shouted from his porch.

"It's fine," Viv said, waving him off. "Maddie, is it?"

The child nodded and backed off a step. It occurred to Viv that it must have taken a lot of courage for the kid to ask the question. Coming up to the scary lady that yelled a lot wasn't exactly easy.

"You want to play with Max?" she asked, keeping her voice soft.

The child nodded, eyes wide.

Viv thought for a second, then said: "Wait here, okay?"

She went into the house. "Max!" He came trotting straight out of the kitchen and she knelt down to clip his leash on. "Want to meet some new friends, Max?"

His tail thumped on the floor and Viv grinned, leading him out of the house.

"I don't think Max has ever played with kids before," she said. "So we'd best be careful. Put your hand out slowly and see if he'll let you pet him."

The wide-eyed child put out a trembling hand and Max immediately swamped it with a hundred licks a minute. The child started to laugh and then Viv did too.

"You want to take him for a walk?" she asked, handing the leash over. "Just on the sidewalk in front of my house and in front of your grandpa's, okay? Not on the street."

The child nodded earnestly and took Max off as Mr. Webber

stepped over the property line.

"You didn't have to do that," he said. "But it was kind. Maddie loves animals. She's been after her mom for months to get a dog, but my daughter's far too busy for things like that."

"You should have said something, Max loves a walk."

Webber eyed her. "And you'd have let Maddie take him?"

"Probably not," Viv agreed. "But now she can, if she wants to."

"I'll tell her. She'll be delighted." He watched his grand-daughter proudly lead Max up and down the sidewalk. "You an animal lover too?" he asked.

Viv grinned. "You know, I really wasn't. But Max has grown on me. I couldn't imagine not having a dog now."

"Huh, shame."

"Why?"

He shrugged. "Just that I volunteer down at the animal shelter and they're always looking for people to help out. I mean, if you wanted to. But if you're not a huge animal lover then, well, I guess..."

"No, no," Viv said, the idea suddenly appealing to her. "Actually, that sounds like fun. I'd like to go."

Webber grinned. "Seriously? I usually go on Tuesdays around lunchtime. How about I pick you up and take you down there and I can introduce you around, show you the ropes?"

Viv grinned. "It's a date."

"Psh, I'm far too old for you," Webber said, winking at her. "Besides, I'm thinking you've got bigger fish to fry than me. Like that blonde lady that used to come by all the time."

"Alice?"

"That her name? You and her were an item, right?"

Viv felt a weight in her chest. She concentrated on watching Maddie walking Max. "No," she said, quietly. "We weren't exactly an item." Then she took a deep breath. "But I think we just might become one, as long as I don't screw this up."

CHAPTER THIRTY FOUR

Viv handed Max's leash over. "Thank you so much."

"It's no problem at all," Webber said. "We'll enjoy having Max stay with us for the evening. And you're looking very nice, if I may say so."

Viv felt herself blush. "Thank you."

"Bit dressy for a book sale, isn't it?" he asked, innocently.

"Well, it's a little more than a book sale," she said, heart beating furiously in her chest.

A little more? A whole hell of a lot more. Only her chance to regain herself, her chance to perhaps start something new and shiny and better, her chance to finally test out the new her that had been in development.

"Going after the girl, are we?" Webber asked with a grin.

"Something like that," said Viv, blushing again.

"I'll tell you something," said Webber.

Not more advice. Her head was swimming with advice. She steeled herself to listen politely. She wasn't taking advice on this matter any more, she was sure of her own head and what she wanted and that was what mattered. What mattered was that she knew she had to give this a chance, whatever the circumstances, whatever Alice's answer was.

"What's that?"

"You can't go wrong with a burger after a night of drinking."

Viv blinked. "Sorry, what?"

"The grease soaks up the booze. It's a sound plan, trust me. If you're going to have a few tonight, get a burger on your way home. You'll thank me for it tomorrow."

"I thought you were going to give me advice about getting the girl," Viv laughed.

He snorted. "I'm an old man with grandchildren running around, what the hell do I know about getting the girl? The last time I got a girl she gave me the clap. Now, off with you, and don't worry about Max."

Viv was still laughing as she walked down the driveway.

❋ ❋ ❋

"It's a bit much, isn't it?" Alice said, doubtfully.

Harrison stood back to admire the red dress. "Not at all. You want to make a splash, right?"

"Yeah, I'm not sure about that."

"Like hell you're not." Harrison straightened up. "Listen to me, I get why you approaching Viv might not be the best plan in the world. But there's no harm in having her approach you, is there?"

Alice swallowed down the sick feeling in her stomach. Sick because there was nothing more that she wanted than for Viv to approach her, for Viv to give them a second chance.

Oh, she had no right to expect it, not after being the one to walk away. And she had no right to ask for it, not when she'd already compromised Viv's stability by sleeping with her in the first place and then leaving her.

But that didn't mean she didn't want it.

"What if she's not there?" The question came out smaller and more quietly than she'd expected.

"You wanted to go with fate on this one, Al," Harrison said. "What happens will happen and all that."

"It's the only way to do it. I can only control so much."

Harrison laughed. "Sorry? Is that Alice? Have you seen my roommate anywhere?"

"What?" Alice asked, irritated enough that her cheeks were turning pink in the mirror.

"You finally admitting that you can't control everything. You can't organize everything. You can't decide that you're just going to be married by the time you're thirty, or whatever the plan was. I think that counts as change, Al, like it or not."

"It had better," Alice said, taking a last long look in the mirror and thinking about the website she'd just commissioned and the new client she was supposed to meet on Monday.

"Change is a way of life," Harrison said.

"I might employ you to write motivational slogans for the business," Alice warned her.

"I have a job, remember?" Harrison smirked. "And it's really time for you to go, you're going to be late."

Alice took a deep breath and tore herself away from the mirror. "I don't know if this is a good idea."

"Then stay at home."

"Harrison!"

Harrison put her hands on her hips. "Alice Knowles, get out of this damn apartment right now or I will throw you out."

"That's not much better," grumbled Alice, getting her purse.

Harrison stopped her as she got to the door. "Al, good luck. Whatever happens. You know as well as I do that you can't force these things. Maybe you're right, if it's meant to happen, then it will. If not, well, you have a business to grow, you have friends, you have a fantastic roommate. Not all will be lost."

Alice nodded, knowing that she was right but terrified nevertheless.

She couldn't base everything around Viv, she knew that. But that wasn't going to stop her being heart-broken if Viv wasn't there. Just seeing her would be enough, she promised herself. She didn't need any more than that.

Viv speaking to her, wanting to be friends even, that was more than she dared dream of.

As for anything else...

Her heart skipped a beat as she went downstairs to find her Uber.

❉ ❉ ❉

"Be careful, you don't want to get book dust on that fancy jacket," Cal said.

"Hey, dressing up like this was your idea," said Viv, putting a book she'd been inspecting down.

"A very fine idea, if I do say so," said Cal with a grin. "There's nothing more romantic than reminding someone of the first time they looked at you with love."

"Yeah, I'm kind of taking your word on that one. You were the one watching her watching me. I'm not so sure that love would be the right word there."

"Oh, trust me," Cal said. "I'm a librarian, we know everything, didn't you know that? And Alice definitely looked at you with love in that outfit." She paused for a second, book in hand. "Or was it lust?"

Viv growled at her.

"Maybe it doesn't matter," Cal said with another wide grin.

"You know, for someone who's closing up her job and selling off the library's books, you're pretty cheerful tonight."

Cal straightened a pile of books. "Don't let appearances fool you. I'm breaking inside," she said.

Viv put a hand on her arm. "It must be hard."

"It is," Cal said. "But it's also necessary. I'm clearing the way for the next step, that's all. I have to see things that way." She sniffed, then smiled again. "I got a job offer, did I tell you?"

"Already?" Viv said.

"The local community college is looking for a librarian. Not a head librarian, like I was here, but it's a far bigger library."

Viv smiled. The library door opened and her head turned as though on a stick. But a young couple walked in and she turned back to Cal. "Congrats, that sounds great. As it happens, I might have a little project myself."

"You?" Cal asked. "Well, isn't that nice? What are you going to be doing?"

"It's nothing big," Viv said. Half her attention on the door. "But the animal shelter needs someone to do a little PR work for them, arranging ads, that sort of thing, so I stepped in."

"Excellent news," said Cal. "We'll have to celebrate. Why don't you and Alice come over to dinner? We can all have a good old gossip and open a bottle of nice wine."

Viv's heart swelled and tightened like a drum. "You're assuming that Alice is going to want to do anything with me," she said quietly.

"Without hope, what is there?" Cal asked, noisily rummaging in a box. "I'll assume the best until I hear differently. I strongly suggest you do the same."

"Wait, aren't you supposed to assume the worst so that you're always pleasantly surprised?"

Cal huffed and shook her head. "What kind of life would that be? Constantly going around thinking negative thoughts all the time? Life's short, my dear, don't waste it with negativity. The chances of coming up heads are the same as the chances of coming up tails, you know."

The door opened again. This time it was a family, two kids, husband and wife hand in hand. Viv's heart was ready to explode.

"Cal?"

"Mmm?"

"What if she doesn't come?"

"Were you not listening to what I literally just said?" Cal said, standing up straight and putting her hands on her hips. Then she paused, mouth half-open until Viv turned to see what she was staring at.

Alice.

Alice in the same red dress outlined in the light by the open door.

Alice, her hair dancing on her shoulders.

Alice.

Viv swallowed, but somehow couldn't take a breath, couldn't do anything other than look.

Cal put a hand on her arm. "Why don't you go find yourself somewhere quiet?" she whispered. "I'm sure Alice will find you."

In a rush, the air became breathable again, her muscles could move, Viv nodded, tearing her eyes away from Alice, rushing off behind the bookshelves.

Just as she had before, hiding away.

But this time was going to be different.

CHAPTER
THIRTY FIVE

A lice spotted Cal behind one of the tables and made her way over, extremely conscious of the fact that she was way overdressed. Her uncomfortable feeling wasn't helped when Cal burst into laughter the second she saw her.

"What?" Alice asked, skin feeling prickly.

"Nothing, my dear, something about great minds thinking alike, is all," said Cal. "Oh, you'll find out, so don't pout. Can I assume that you're looking for Viv?"

Alice let out a breath that she felt like she'd been holding for weeks. "Is she here?"

Cal nodded. "In what's becoming her usual place," she said. She eyed Alice for a moment. "Have you decided what you want?"

Alice looked down at the table full of books and Cal laughed again.

"I'm not talking about books," she said. "I'm talking about Viv."

Alice put up a hand to stop her talking. "I know she's vulnerable. I know I have no right to come back, I know—"

"Psh," Cal interrupted. "She's no more vulnerable than I am, you neither for that matter. All I'm asking is if you're here for a reason. And if you are, and you look like you are, then go on back and find her. Let's get this story finished before I have to close this whole damn place down."

Her hands were shaky. She only realized just now that her hands were shaky and her legs didn't feel right either. And her mouth was dry.

Cal grinned at her and gestured with her head toward the bookshelves in the corner and it was almost as though the past was happening all over again.

Slowly, Alice walked toward the shelves, pushed her way between them, toward the quiet corner where she'd first kissed Viv.

And there she was, leaning up against the shelves in that suit with the heels that made her legs stretch on forever, with her mouth swollen and her hair slicked back and a shiver of delight went through Alice's core.

She knew.

Right in that moment, she knew.

This was her ending. This was what fate was dealing her. This was the happiness she hadn't known that she wanted.

* * *

"We're changing things up." Viv's voice came out as more of a growl than she expected. But she deliberately didn't move, didn't take a step forward.

"We are?" Alice said, light sparkling in her hair.

"This time we talk first and kiss later," said Viv. Which was awfully presumptive of her but every fear she'd had had just jumped out of the window.

Alice was here. Alice was perfect. Alice was wearing that red dress and had come to find her. It was the final piece of the jigsaw puzzle and all Viv needed to do was slot it back into place.

"Viv, I—"

"No," Viv said. "You let me talk first. I need to get this out and I need to be the one who says it, not you."

Alice nodded, putting one hand on a shelf to steady herself.

Here goes nothing, Viv thought, trying to order the words in her head.

"You're not my life coach any more," she said. "And I know that you're used to being right. Hell, you're always right about everything. Except this. You made a mistake, Alice. A huge one."

"What's that?"

"I realized it's all about change, you see," Viv said. Her hands were aching to reach out and touch Alice, but she didn't quite dare. "You think I'm afraid of change, and maybe you were right, once. But not anymore, Alice. Because I'm standing right here and I'm willing to change. Not for you, you understand, but because of you. Do you see the difference?"

Alice swallowed and Viv couldn't help but push herself off the shelf and take a tiny step toward her.

"I'm not what you wanted, I can see that. I'm older than you, I'm grumpy and set in my ways. I'm divorced and, frankly, the idea of marriage makes me feel slightly sick. I'm nothing you've ever wanted in your life, right? Even you couldn't see yourself getting married to me, you said so."

"Viv..."

"No, let me finish," Viv said, a baby step closer. "The thing is, you're not what I wanted either. Do you think I wanted Little Miss Sunshine walking into my life and turning it all upside down again? Do you think I wanted someone who all of a sudden had me even considering the idea of marriage again? Of course I didn't."

A little closer. Close enough that she could smell Alice's perfume, flowery and sweet, enough to make her feel drunk.

"But I think that's kind of the point, that we're neither a perfect dream match. I think that's where you stumble in your argument about me hating change. Because you're no fan of it yourself, are you, Alice?"

A small smile.

"Here's you and I, both wanting something we never thought we'd want and both trying to pull away from it for a bunch of stupid reasons. When really, all this takes is for both of us to change together. Isn't that what a relationship should be? One partner making the other a better person, a stronger person."

Another step closer.

Viv had to take a deep, steadying breath.

"I can see how you make me a better person, Alice. What I'm not so sure about is how I make you better, how you're better with me than you would be alone."

Alice looked at the ground. "I'm starting my own business. As a life coach. Going back to school, getting some qualifications. I'd never have done that without you, Viv."

"Okay," Viv said, close enough now that they could almost touch. "So we can change each other, improve each other. That's a pretty powerful argument. But there is something else."

"What's that?"

The book sale went on behind them, chatter and the clinking of coins. But just for a moment, this little corner was the very center of the world, the center of a ball that was the only still, stable point in the universe.

Knowing that this was what had to happen, that she had to take the last step, Viv smiled. Alice's blue eyes looked up at her, and she stopped restraining herself, stopped trying to read things, analyze things, stopped thinking or worrying or anything else.

As she leaned in, Alice's face tilted up toward her and Viv's heart pounded in her chest until their lips touched and her hands came up to cradle Alice's face.

Then she pulled away. Because she had to. Because one millisecond longer and there'd be no turning back. Because Alice had a say in this too.

"There's this," she said hoarsely. "The way you make me feel, the way I want to not just change myself but change the world for you. The way I want to wake up next to you every morning and go to sleep in your arms every night. The way I can't imagine a world without you in it, even if that means having to let you go to find your happiness elsewhere."

She dropped her hands, stepped back.

"Because I will, Alice, if that's what you need. I'll walk away right now. And if that's not proof of me changing, I don't know what is. I swear to you that I'll go and I'll get on with my life. Just say the word."

It felt like a long time, far longer than it really was. Viv could hear someone arguing about a book, a child begging his mother for something. She heard Cal laugh somewhere and someone ask where the bathroom was.

But her eyes were on Alice's beautiful, delicate face.

"Can I say something now?" Alice asked.

Viv bit her lip and nodded.

"You're the grumpiest, most stubborn person I've ever met," Alice said. "You can be rude, dark, isolated. But for some reason, I can't stay away from you."

Viv's stomach somersaulted. "You—"

Alice put a hand on her cheek. "No, you let me finish now. We were both looking for something. But maybe we didn't know exactly what we were looking for. I don't know why I want this, I don't know if it will work, I don't know anything except one thing."

Viv let out a breath. "Which is?"

"I'm afraid I'm going to scare you."

"More than a fucking bungee jump?" Viv couldn't help but burst out.

Alice laughed. "Yes, more than a bungee jump."

"I'd better hold on then," said Viv, pulling Alice into her arms and holding tight. "Okay, I'm ready. Go ahead."

Alice cleared her throat. "Viv, I think I might be falling in love with you."

"Wow," Viv said, already starting to nuzzle into Alice's neck. "That's the most terrifying thing I've ever heard."

"I told you so," Alice said, beginning to lose her breath as Viv slid a hand down over her hipbone.

"Wanna hear something equally scary?"

"Mm-hmm," said Alice, apparently no longer capable of speech as Viv's kisses descended to her collarbone.

"I think that I possibly, just might be, maybe, falling in love with you too."

Which was the last thing either one of them said for a very, very long time.

EPILOGUE

Alice pulled out the party platter and stowed it on the kitchen table while she pulled yet more Tupperware out of the refrigerator.

"Why are we doing this?" Viv grumbled. She was up to her elbows in dishwashing water.

"We have to tell people," Alice said, beginning to arrange celery sticks and carrot batons. "I mean, they're going to notice sooner or later."

"I know that," said Viv. "What I meant is why the hell are we having them all over to the house?"

"Because we live here and inviting people into your home is important for building intimacy," Alice said absently.

Viv growled at her. "You take this life coaching thing too far sometimes. I'm not a client."

Alice wiggled her eyebrows. "You were a client though. And sometimes I like to remind you of just how we met."

There was a gurgle as Viv pulled the plug from the sink, then she reached for a towel to dry her arms. "Start talking like that and there'll be consequences," she said.

"Is that a threat or a promise?" Alice wiped off her own hands and came over to the sink, looping her arms around Viv's waist. "Stop being so grumpy."

"I can't help it. It's a lot to handle, there's a lot going on. And then you're running around fixing party food like Betsy Ross and

—"

"Betsy Ross? Um, Betty Crocker maybe?" Alice said, face crumpled into a frown.

"What's the difference?"

"One sewed the first American flag, the other makes cupcakes." Alice was biting her lip to keep from laughing.

"Yeah, I meant the cupcake one. And you shouldn't be doing all this stuff. You're exhausted, what, with the grant proposal and all the presentations you've been doing."

Viv sighed and looked down into Alice's clear blue eyes. She really had been working too hard. The life coaching business had taken off immediately, just as Viv had always known it would. But that wasn't enough for Alice.

She'd come up with a plan to start a training course for people who wanted to be coaches themselves. She said it was her way of standardizing the process, saving the world from charlatans like Foster Davison.

"The grant proposal was turned in three weeks ago and there are no more investment presentations to make," Alice said. "Now I just wait for the results. Either I get the funding or I don't."

"And what will you do if you don't?"

"I will," grinned Alice.

"Alright, Little Miss Sunshine."

"Viv, stop worrying. I can set my own limits and I can more than handle what I've got on my plate, okay?"

"It's not like I'm contributing so much," Viv said, feeling the weight of guilt in her stomach. "I mean, I can't jump in and save you like Harrison used to do, paying all the bills."

"You pay more than your share of the bills, we live in your house," Alice pointed out. "Besides, you're going to be busy enough sooner rather than later, so maybe you should enjoy this calm before the storm, don't you think?"

"Hmmph."

"Really? You're going to 'hmmph' me?"

Viv felt a grin creeping across her face. "You did promise

consequences if I kept being grumpy," she said, hands already wandering down Alice's spine.

Alice gave a delicious shiver and was leaning in for a kiss when the doorbell rang. "Guests already," she shrieked, jumping out of Viv's arms.

"At least we know it's not Evie," Viv said. "Since it's someone polite enough to use the bell."

Max was already sitting patiently by the front door and Viv patted his head as she opened up, letting in Mr. Webber, his grandson in his arms, and Maddie, who was officially Max's favorite person in the world.

❋ ❋ ❋

"So, is he the one?" Alice asked, eyeing the tall young man whose name she'd unfortunately forgotten.

Harrison rolled her eyes. "For real, Al? Stop trying to marry everyone off. Charlie's cool, I like him, but it's way too early to say anything like that."

"I'm not sure he thinks so," Alice said, watching as he bounced Evie's son Ollie on his knees.

"He's the oldest of like six kids, he's used to being around babies," Harrison said dismissively. "Now, I want to know why we're all here. What's the big secret?"

"You'll find out along with everyone else," Alice said.

"I'm your best friend, you have to tell me!"

"Just wait a little while longer, you'll find out. How's work?"

"Fine, great, wonderful. I got a promotion."

"Another one?"

"I'm looking at hitting VP by the time I'm forty," Harrison said. She looked at the glass of wine in Alice's hand. "Hmm. You're not pregnant. That can't be the secret. And there's no way Viv would consent to getting married, so it's not that either."

"Stop playing detective," said Alice. "If you want to be helpful, then go see if anyone needs a drink refill."

"I can't believe you're putting me to work here."

Alice grinned, but as Harrison was about to walk away she put a hand on her arm. "He's a nice guy," she said, knowing full well that Harrison hated hoping that things would work out, hated putting all her eggs in one basket.

"I know," said Harrison, with a half-smile. "I'll tell you a secret: I actually really like this one."

Alice squeezed her arm. "Then don't let him run away. If you don't tell him you like him, how is he supposed to know?"

Harrison snorted and shook her arm free. "I'll make sure he knows," she said. "Don't you worry about that."

Alice laughed as Harrison went off to find more wine.

* * *

"Fuck me, he's strong," Viv gasped as her godson gripped tight onto her finger.

"Viv, don't swear in front of Ollie," Evie said.

"As if he understands," said Greg. "Besides, I've heard you say way worse."

Evie pulled a face at him and Viv laughed then grimaced. "Jesus, things aren't smelling great around here. Please tell me that isn't you, Greg."

"Ha ha, very funny," Greg said, lifting his son out of Viv's arms. "Come on, soldier, let's get you changed."

"No," Ollie said.

Viv raised an eyebrow at Evie who shrugged. "It's his new word. And believe me, he makes the most of it."

"No, no, no," Ollie sang as Greg carted him away for a diaper change.

"Isn't that lovely. The perfect caring husband, finally."

"Oh Viv, don't be such a bitch. Or a hypocrite. I know damn well that you and Greg have been playing that stupid video game online until all hours at night. Besides, you can't deny that Greg has been the perfect dad. I think it's time that you admitted that you actually like him."

"Huh," was all Viv said, knowing that Evie was right.

"And it's about time you let us all in on this secret that you guys have. You know we're dying to know."

"You're one to talk about keeping secrets, you'll find out soon."

Evie rolled her eyes. "I swear, Viv..."

"No, no, no, no interfering best friend nonsense today. The big announcement is coming any minute now. Alice is probably just waiting for Greg to finish changing Ollie."

"Interfering best friend nonsense, my ass," Evie said. "Don't you forget that your interfering best friend found you the perfect life partner."

Viv couldn't help but grin. "You might have a point there."

"And don't you forget it," Evie said, laughing.

* * *

"Be careful," Cal said as Lea casually slid the cake onto the tray.

"I made the thing," Lea said. "I know how to treat cake. Stop interfering."

"I'm your wife, it's my job to interfere," Cal said, grinning. She turned to Viv and Alice. "You girls ready for this?"

"Alice said we have to be," Viv grumbled. "She said people will notice sooner or later so we have to tell them. Though why the hell we had to make a big announcement with cake and everything, I don't know."

"Because this is an event to celebrate," Alice said. "It's something we want to remember."

Viv squeezed her hand and Alice relaxed just a little. Even after all this time it was occasionally difficult to tell when Viv was being seriously grumpy and when she was just having an attitude about something.

Max barked and then ran through the kitchen, closely followed by Maddy who skidded to a halt when she saw the adults.

"Hello, Ms. Sunshine," she said politely to Alice. "And hello, Ms. Grumpy," to Viv. Then she bolted off after Max.

"You actually let her call you that?" Cal asked.

Viv shrugged. "You can't tell a kid off for telling the truth," she said.

"Oh, you'd be surprised, as I'm sure you're about to find out," Cal said.

Alice looked down at the cake. It was beautiful. Lea had done a fantastic job. She and Cal were the only ones that already knew, and only because Alice had wanted one of Lea's amazing cakes for the announcement.

"Come on," Lea said to Cal. "Let's go and sit in the living room. I'm pretty sure Viv and Al can carry this thing in by themselves."

They disappeared, leaving Alice and Viv alone.

"You ready?" Viv asked.

Alice reached out for her hand. "Are you?"

"Nope," said Viv with a grin. "But when are we ever ready for change? We face it, deal with it, and incorporate it, right?"

"You've been reading my hand-outs again."

Her breath was coming a little faster and her legs felt wobbly. Viv noticed and pulled her in for a hug. "We're ready," she whispered. "So let's go tell everybody how ready we are, okay?"

"You'll carry the cake?" Alice asked, aware that her hands were shaking far too much to carry something so precious.

Viv picked the tray up. "Cake carried, come on, Little Miss Sunshine, let's do this. There's antsy people out there who don't like secrets."

Alice laughed as she followed Viv into the living room.

"Ooo, cake," Maddie said as soon as they walked through the door.

The adults started chattering and standing up and Evie was the one who leaned over to see the frosting.

"'We're Approved'," she said, frowning. "For what? A mortgage?"

"Nope, they own the house," Mr. Webber said. "I'm sure of that."

"Maybe it's a car loan or something," Greg said helpfully.

"Jesus, why don't you give them a chance to tell you?" said Cal.

Alice cleared her throat as Viv put the cake down on the coffee table where both Ollie and Max eyed it.

"We've been approved by the adoption agency that we registered with," she said, voice hardly shaking at all.

And then she was engulfed in hugs and kisses, but her hand remained firmly in Viv's as everyone cheered.

"When?" Evie shouted out.

Viv grinned. "It might be tomorrow, it might be six months from now, we really can't say. But soon, they've promised us that."

"They said we'd make the perfect parents," Alice put in, anxious that everyone should know that.

"Well, that's obvious," Harrison said.

And then there was a very long and complicated discussion about child-rearing and naming and discipline and a million other things that Alice barely listened to. Because her eyes were fixed on Viv, smiling and answering questions and looking as beautiful as she always did.

"I'm lucky," Alice murmured to herself. "So lucky."

Viv looked up and caught her eye, flashing her a smile that was just for her, and Alice smiled back.

❊ ❊ ❊

It was late in the evening, the dusk already setting in, by the time everyone had left and Viv and Alice were sitting out on the deck, glasses in hands.

"Well, that was quite the party. Damn hard work though," Viv said.

"It was the first time in two years that we've done that," said Alice.

Viv grunted. "Let's wait another two years before we do it again."

"Grumpy."

"Isn't that why you love me?"

Alice laughed. "Maybe it is.

The last birds were singing and the fireflies were starting to come out and in the blink of an eye the moment was there.

Not that she hadn't been thinking about it. Thinking about it and doubting it and wondering if she would ever be ready again. Except now she was. From one moment to the next.

"I've been thinking," she said.

"Mmm?" Alice said, looking out over the deck and sipping her wine.

"We should get married." The words kind of blurted out and Viv started shaking the second they'd been said. Not because she regretted them but because the carefully prepared speech she'd thought of hadn't come to her mind at all.

Alice turned slowly to look at her, the breeze stirring her blonde hair. "Married?"

Viv nodded and looked down at her hands, trying to regain some of the rehearsed words from her head. "It's just..."

"Viv, you don't have to—"

"No, I want to," Viv said, steeling herself and looking back at Alice. "Here's the thing. I love you. I love you with all my heart and we're going to have a kid together, maybe more than one, and I don't want you to ever, ever walk away again."

"I'm not going anywhere," Alice said, a small smile tickling at the corner of her lips.

"Then I'll make sure of it by signing legal papers."

Alice laughed. "It's really not necessary, Viv. I love you too, but this, all this, it's all already so perfect."

Viv sighed. "I don't have to, Al. But I want to. Here's the thing. I want to see you walk down the aisle toward me, I want to see you all dressed in white, I want everyone, all our friends and family, to see me promise to devote my life to you. I truly, honestly want this."

"Why now?" Alice asked.

"I have no idea. I think maybe it's just taken me this long to realize that that's actually what I want, that I'm not just doing it because I think you want it."

She put her wine glass down and stood up.

"I should have done this properly," she said, preparing to get down on her knees.

But Alice stood up and took both her hands, pulling her in. "You did it properly," she said.

"Yeah, I'm pretty sure that's not winning any awards for most romantic proposals."

Alice laughed. "Maybe not. But it was perfect for me."

There was a silence and Viv could feel Alice's heart beating, could smell her now familiar scent, could feel the warmth of her body, and she had a strange fizzing feeling in her stomach. The fizzing that she always got when Alice was near, even now.

Alice leaned in for a kiss, but Viv pulled back.

"Um, you didn't exactly answer me."

"To be fair, you didn't exactly ask me a question," Alice whispered. "It was a statement. I thought everything was decided already." She smiled.

"Has anyone ever told you that you smile too much?"

"Frequently," Alice said. "And just so you know, I'd be honored to be your wife."

THANKS FOR READING!

If you liked this book, why not leave a review?
Reviews are so important to independent
authors, they help new readers discover
us, and give us valuable feedback. Every
review is very much appreciated.

And if you want to stay up to date with the latest
Sienna Waters news and new releases, then follow
me on Twitter or on Facebook, or check me out at:

www.siennawaters.com

Keep reading for a sneak peek of my next book!

BOOKS FROM SIENNA WATERS

The Oakview Series:

The Monday's Child Series:

The Hawkin Island Series:

Standalone Books:

Or turn the page to get a sneak preview of **Crossing the Pond**

CROSSING THE POND

Chapter One

"**T**ry to see this as an opportunity."

Ted Scanlon attempted what could be called a smile and Piper kind of wanted to punch him. Not that she would, but she wanted to.

Fifteen years of devoting her life to this stupid, lousy job and getting fired was supposed to be an opportunity?

An opportunity to do what exactly?

"Maybe I'll raise trick goldfish for the carnival," she muttered, not quite as under her breath as she'd thought, since Scanlon raised his eyebrows in surprise.

"Well, uh, that's certainly one possibility," he said. He cleared his throat. "You'll get all the normal benefits, of course." He slid a piece of paper across his desk to her. "A generous severance package, health insurance until the end of the year, glowing references." That half-assed attempt at a smile again.

Piper wondered if she'd ever actually seen him really smile. Maybe not, now that she thought of it. He'd only be around for a half year or so though, not enough time to really fit into the Foster and Davis family.

"Please understand, Ms. Garland, this isn't personal."

How could having her job snatched away not be personal? Piper's jaw ached as she tried to keep her mouth shut.

"The publishing business has been going through a hard time, there are a lot of lay-offs here, it's just unfortunate that you're one of them. We at Foster and Davis really do appreciate all you've done for the company."

Which was about as much as she could take.

She slid the paper off the table, crumpled it and shoved it into a pocket, and stood up to leave.

And because she'd worked professionally for fifteen years, and because she knew she needed the severance settlement and health insurance, and because she was a grown damned adult and not an impulsive child, she smiled. "Thank you," she said, before she walked out.

Even though she still really, really wanted to punch him.

She could have gone back to her desk. She could have collected all her things, the manuscripts and desk ornaments and awards and everything else. Instead, she patted her pockets to make sure she had her wallet and walked right out the door.

Because despite being professional and an adult and all the rest, and despite it only being three o'clock in the afternoon, she really, really needed a drink. A big one. With umbrellas and at least three different colors and enough chunks of fruit around the rim of the glass that it was almost impossible to drink.

"THINK OF IT as an opportunity?"

"Uh-huh," Piper said, sucking up her second cocktail through a chunky straw.

"What an asshole." The bartender smiled sweetly at her and grabbed the cocktail shaker. "Here, let me make you another, this one's on me."

Piper, who had been planning to leave after two, shrugged. Why the hell not? It wasn't like she had work tomorrow.

The bartender flashed her a pretty smile. Actually, all of her was pretty, not just the smile. Pretty and young, she couldn't be more than twenty or so. Piper sighed and tucked a lock of blonde hair back behind her ear.

Young enough that she had her whole life ahead of her. The thought made Piper feel vaguely nauseous.

"Actually, thanks for the offer, but I'd better be going." Before she made a fool of herself.

"Oh," the bartender flushed. "Oh, sure, no problem." She bent and scribbled something on a napkin. "Uh, here you go."

"What's that?" Piper asked, taking the napkin.

"My number."

Piper chuckled. "That's sweet, but I'm fine, really. I've only had two drinks, I'm perfectly safe to get home, but you're lovely to be concerned." She put a ten dollar bill on the bar next to the napkin as a tip and slipped off her bar stool. "You have a good evening."

She was more than half way home before she realized that perhaps the sweet young bartender hadn't been concerned about her getting home. More concerned with getting her home. Then she groaned and put her sunglasses on.

Could this day get any worse?

"THINK OF IT as a fucking opportunity?" Joey shrieked down the phone. "Seriously?"

"I know, I know," said Piper, opening the fridge door and surveying the contents.

"An opportunity to do what?"

"Travel the world with money I don't have? Get out of the city? Become a stripper or a mechanic? The possibilities are endless." She selected a yogurt that was only two days past the date stamped on the lid.

There was the sound of a sigh rattling down the phone line. "Pipes, you want me to come over?"

"No, I'm fine." An adult, a professional, very able to take care of myself, Piper's brain said. Despite the fact that she kind of wanted to sit on the bathroom floor and cry. "Besides, I have plans. Sitting on the bathroom floor and crying is at the top of the list of my priorities right now."

"Yeah, I kind of feel like I should come."

Piper peeled the foil off the top of the yogurt then sat on the floor to eat. She hadn't had time to buy a sofa. Now she didn't have money to buy a sofa, so it was probably just as well that she hadn't had time.

"No, really," she said, dipping her spoon into the yogurt. "I'm two big drinks down, I'm eating yogurt on the floor of my still unfurnished apartment, I'm not exactly at my best."

"I'm your best friend, I'm not sure that stuff matters."

"You're my only friend, currently," Piper pointed out, stirring the yogurt.

"That can't possibly be true."

"It is. I lost most of the others in the break-up. Then the rest will go with the job I've just lost. Which leaves you."

Joey snorted. "Bullshit. Okay, maybe the work stuff is true. But as for everyone else, well, they just feel kind of awkward, I guess. Like most people do after a big break up. They don't know what to say. Reach out to them, they'll be fine."

"I don't think I've got the energy." She put a spoon of yogurt in her mouth and promptly spit it back out into the pot. "Eugh."

"What?"

"Yogurt's gone bad."

"How can you tell? Isn't yogurt just bad milk or something?"

"Your culinary knowledge is extraordinary," Piper said, putting the yogurt down and leaning back against the kitchen cabinets. "I don't want to reach out. I kind of don't want to be reminded of Lex, if I'm being honest."

"Understandable. Breaking up after a decade isn't easy."

"No, more because I still sort of want to slap her. I mean, cheating on me with a student, how clichéd can you get?"

"Lucky she's a college professor and not a middle school teacher," Joey said.

"Bad taste, Joe."

"Right, sorry." There was a pause. "Sure you don't want me to come over?"

Piper sighed. "I think I'm just going to go to bed."

"It's quarter to seven."

"So? I'm thirty six years old, my partner has left me, I've lost my job, and the only thing to eat in my refrigerator is out-of-date yogurt, which doesn't matter since I don't have any furniture to sit on to eat anyway. An early night sounds like it might be a good idea, under the circumstances."

"No need to get snappy," Joey said. "But, yeah, I get your point. Listen, how about I pick you up tomorrow and we get drinks? My treat?"

Piper softened. She did want to see Joey, there was a reason they were best friends, after all. Joey's smile was contagious and right now that seemed like the only way Piper was going to get a smile, by catching it off someone else.

"Yeah, okay. I'll call you in the afternoon, okay?"

She hung up, putting her mobile into her pocket, standing up and looking over the kitchen. She really might just as well go to bed. There was no TV, no food, and her laptop was in the bedroom where at least there was a bed.

She'd soothe herself with old episodes of The Golden Girls until she fell asleep.

She was about to go when she caught sight of the mail on the counter where she'd left it. Probably bills and junk, but she might as well get it over with. It wasn't like her day could get any worse.

Three offers for super fast internet, one flyer for a Chinese restaurant, and one electricity bill later, she was left with only one envelope to open.

Scowling down at it she wondered if this was really for her. The envelope was heavy, not because it was too full, but because the paper was thick and good quality. The stamp in the upper corner was unfamiliar, larger than she was used to. She flipped the letter over and saw the return address.

Huh.

The United Kingdom.

She flipped it back, double-checking that it really was her name on the front.

Yep, no doubt there. Her name alright. And her old address

scratched out, the new one written in a cramped hand that she knew wasn't Lex's. Maybe it was that student of hers. Piper's stomach hurt at the very idea.

She grabbed a knife from the sink, wiped it off on her pants and slid it under the flap. This envelope was too nice to open with her fingernails, too nice to be ripped. She up-ended it and a thick letter fell out.

Weirdly, her fingers trembled as she opened it. She read the address one more time.

"Where the fuck is Sutton's Walk?" she murmured.

Then she frowned as she read down the rest of the letter.

CHAPTER TWO

Cam's spade hit something hard and she grunted, wriggling the blade until it got under the stone and she could heave it up.

Sweat was collecting in the small of her back and she was dying for a drink. But she'd promised herself that she'd dig over the whole flower bed first, and she always kept her promises.

'There's nothing worse than a broken heart except a broken promise,' her mother always said. So her mouth was going to stay dry until she was done.

"What you doing out there, girl?"

Cam groaned inwardly, then stood up, stretching out her back. "Digging up the flower beds, Arthur," she called back.

Arthur Slater peered over the fence and sniffed. "No point in doing that now, is there? Not now that Her Highness has popped her clogs. Ain't no one to pay you."

Which was all too true, not that Cam cared to think too much about it. Lucy Cromwell had upped and died two months ago, done her shopping in the morning, come home for lunch, and was dead by tea-time. Not that it should be that surprising, what, with her being all of ninety-eight. Still, she'd been a sprightly ninety-eight.

Which shouldn't excuse the fact that Cam had, technically, signed a contract with a woman on death's doorstep, but still. Lucy Cromwell had been a village institution in Sutton's Walk, it had been hard to imagine the place without her until she was gone.

"Got to keep the place looking nice," she said now. "There'll be a new owner soon enough."

"One of them city types, I reckon," Arthur said. "Or a tourist. Someone with a wad of cash to spend, anyways." His eyes narrowed. "Which is why you're doing what you're doing, I suppose."

Cam's face prickled with heat. "What's that supposed to mean then?"

"That you're putting in the extra work in the hopes that you get noticed and the new owners take you on," he said.

Which again, was all too true, but Cam really didn't feel like confirming it. Not when Arthur was the village gossip and not altogether charitable at the best of times. She picked up her spade again.

"It'll do you no good. They'll hire one of the big companies, not a slip of a girl like you," Arthur pushed.

"Then let's say I'm doing this for the good of the village," Cam said. "Keeping things looking nice for all of us."

"Huh." Arthur sniffed again and Cam sighed, putting the spade down.

"You doing okay there, Art?"

"Don't call me Art. And I'm fine, just think I might be coming down with something, that's all."

"Want me to get the doctor out for you?"

"No, no, I don't want any fuss. It's probably just a summer cold."

Cam looked at the flower bed she'd been turning over, then the four others that still needed doing. Arthur was right, of course, she was hoping to impress whoever the new owners would be. She needed the work.

Being a female contractor wasn't exactly easy. But more of a problem was the fact that Sutton's Walk was a small village and there just wasn't all that much to do.

In the two months since Lucy Cromwell had died, taking with

her the promise of a hefty renovation contract, Cam had had exactly five call outs. And three of those were for Mrs. Carter's kitchen tap which dripped incessantly. Mostly because her five year old twins used it as a handhold to climb up to the biscuit tin on the shelf above the sink.

Then she looked over again at Arthur, who was no spring chicken himself. "What can I get for you, Arthur?"

"Well, I was just about to go to the shops and get a nice tin of soup for lunch."

She nodded. "Give me ten minutes to finish this bed and then I'll go get it for you."

He beamed a smile that was missing more than one tooth. "Don't forget the bread. And an extra pint of milk wouldn't go amiss either. Oh, and some of that chewy licorice if they've got some in again."

Cam took a deep breath, then nodded and smiled. "Alright, I'll finish up and then go."

"Don't forget to take Billy with you, he could use the walk," Arthur said as he tottered away from the fence and back to his kitchen.

Cam bit her tongue. The rest of the flower beds would have to wait. She wasn't getting paid for them anyway. She leaned back down over her spade. But she did really, really want to re-claim this renovation project. She'd been so close, and the opportunity had just slipped through her fingers.

She sighed and got back to work.

"YOU LOOK JUST about done in," Beth said, banging a cup of tea onto the counter.

It was dark enough to stain the cup, real builder's tea, and it made Cam grin. Beth was just about the most supportive person she knew. Cam was a contractor, so she got builder's tea, just the same as any of the workmen would have gotten.

"I've had better days," she said, picking up the mug gratefully.

"Oh yeah? I thought I saw you over at the Cromwell place?

Didn't know you were a gardener too," said Beth, picking up a tea towel and starting to dry some cups.

"Ha ha, I was just keeping my hand in." She took a sip of tea and it was far too hot. "Not like I had anything else to do today."

Beth pulled a face. "That bad, eh?"

"Kind of," admitted Cam. "And then to top things off I ended up at Arthur's, making him lunch and then looking at his war scrapbooks again."

Beth rolled her eyes and leaned on the counter. "You've got to learn to say no, Cam, seriously. I mean, being nice to an old man is one thing, but just how many times has he dragged you through those scrapbooks?"

"About seven," groaned Cam.

Beth laughed. "You're a glutton for punishment." She reached under the cafe counter. "Here you go, this just came in today."

Cam took the book and then squealed in delight. "Is it gory?"

"Look at the cover, you eejit. There's more blood on there than the shower scene from Carrie, I think it'll fulfill your prurient desires."

Cam clasped the horror book to her chest. "You've made my day."

"Doesn't take much," said Beth.

"It's escapism is all. And after today I could use a little escape. Actually, after the last two months I could use an escape."

Beth pushed over a plate of ginger biscuits. "Go on, take one," she said.

Cam grinned again. Beth was not only the owner and sole staff member of Sutton Walk's only cafe stroke bookshop, she was also the village's unofficial therapist and Cam's best friend. Which meant she knew all about her weakness for ginger biscuits.

"Been thinking about other opportunities?" Beth asked, pulling the plate out of reach after Cam had selected a biscuit, knowing that if she didn't the entire plate would disappear.

Cam shook her head. "I can't do anything else. Building and contracting is what I'm good at. The only other choice would be to move away and I really don't want that."

"None of us want that," Beth said. "But you've got to do something, my love. You can't go around half-unemployed."

"I'm lucky really," said Cam. "I mean, I've got my family, I've got enough to eat and friends and a lovely village."

Beth stood up and put her hands on her hips. "Camilla Fabbri, you live in a van."

Cam took a breath then let it go. "I do."

"You do."

"It's a nice van," Cam said.

"It's a van parked in your parent's farmyard," said Beth. "You're thirty two years old."

"And hardly a success story," groaned Cam, going back to her tea.

Beth leaned on the counter again. "You've got to start putting yourself first, Cam. You're always doing things for other people, always putting your plans on hold, and then you end up losing out. I love that you're generous and giving, but at some point, *you* need to be your priority."

"It's not like I haven't tried."

The Cromwell contract was supposed to be the turning point. A long term job that she could use to prove her worth. The job she'd needed for years, something that would let her really show off her skills, and that would lead to more work down the line.

And the promised cash would come in more than handy. Lucy Cromwell had been sweet, slightly eccentric, and very lovable. She'd also been generous and Cam had had to rein her in when it came to payment, replacing Lucy's unbelievable offer with something a little more reasonable.

Reasonable, but still enough to put down a deposit on a cottage when added to the savings Cam already had.

Now that chance was gone. Unless she could persuade whoever was taking over the house to honor the contract.

"I know you've tried," Beth said, patting her hand. "Your day will come, Cam. I'm just worried that you'll be too busy shopping for Arthur or babysitting your brother's kids or helping me unload boxes of books to realize that it's your day, that's all."

Cam frowned but said nothing. There was no point. Beth was right. She did have a hard time putting herself first. And she didn't think that was a bad thing. She thought, she hoped, it made her a good person, and that was all she really wanted to be.

"Hey, you know it's half past five, don't you?" Beth said looking up at the big clock above the shop door.

"Jesus," said Cam, practically dropping her cup of tea as she scrambled off her stool. "My mum'll kill me."

Dinner was on the big farmhouse table at six sharp and Cam still hadn't showered or even brushed her hair that day now that she came to think about it.

"Run," Beth said, collecting Cam's cup. "You'll make it. Just."

Cam shouted her thanks over her shoulder as she ran out the door. Everything else in her life would just have to wait. No one was late to Mama Fabbri's dinner table. At least not if you wanted to eat.

Get Your Copy of Crossing the Pond Now, Only from Amazon!

Printed in Great Britain
by Amazon

35593105R00126